DISCARDED BY THE LEVI
HEYWOOD MEMORIAL LIBRARY

PATCHSADDLE DRIVE

Also by Cliff Farrell

TREACHERY TRAIL

DEATH TRAP ON THE PLATTE

THE GUNS OF JUDGMENT DAY

COMANCH'

CROSSFIRE

BUCKO

RETURN OF THE LONG RIDERS

RIDE THE WILD COUNTRY

THE WALKING HILLS

THE TRAIL OF THE TATTERED STAR

RIDE THE WILD TRAIL

FORT DECEPTION

THE LEAN RIDER

SANTE FE WAGON BOSS

OWLHOOT TRAIL

Patchsaddle Drive

CLIFF FARRELL

F

F ARR

WEST.

Garden City, New York

DOUBLEDAY & COMPANY, INC.

1972

All of the characters in this book are fictitious, and any resemblance to actual persons, living or dead, is purely coincidental.

11/72 - Dal - 2,)5

ISBN: 0-385-08472-2
Library of Congress Catalog Card Number 72–79386

Copyright © 1972 by Cliff Farrell
All Rights Reserved
Printed in the United States of America
First Edition

PATCHSADDLE DRIVE

CHAPTER 1

Clay Burnet was trying to set down on canvas the dream of tranquillity that was always in his thoughts and which always seemed within reach and yet tantalizingly evaded him. He was peering, frowning, at the sketch, his homemade palette, his homemade brush poised, when, from the corner of an eye, he detected movement in the thickets along the creek.

It might have been a deer or a wild turkey. Clay could not be sure, for the distance was upward of two hundred yards. It could have been only imagination. He laid aside the palette and brush and picked up his rifle. It was a Henry that he had leaned against a pillar of the gallery near at hand.

"Micah!" he called.

"Comin'!" A black man stepped from the nearby kitchen door of the house. He was big and broad, in his middle thirties. He wore rundown, patched boots, a patched butternut shirt, and faded breeches inlaid with leather for saddlework. He read Clay's expression, and, without asking questions, retreated into the house and quickly reappeared with his rifle in his hands. It was a muzzle-loading Sharps which had the initials CSA burned into the stock. Clay's Henry bore the same emblem, but the letters had been branded over the original mark of ownership, which was USA.

Clay waved the muzzle of his weapon in the direction of the creek. "There just below the ford. I thought I saw a rider. Not too sure of it."

"Injun?"

"Could be. No telling. All I got was a squeaky glimpse from half an eye."

He laid the rifle across his knees, picked up the palette and brush again, pretending to resume painting. He eased farther back of the easel, trying to make a smaller target of himself. Micah edged back into the shadow of the doorway. They waited.

The quiet landscape whose beauty Clay had been trying to capture on canvas remained silent in the early afternoon sun. It was late March. The weather had turned mild; the air was laden with the bursting new fragrance of budding greenery and moist earth.

The first section of the new ranch house that Clay and Micah had raised stone by stone, beam by beam, lintel by lintel, stood nearly complete and livable. It was built in the hacienda style, low and rambling, with a roof of crooked red tile that they had packed by mule from the kilns in Mexico. A gallery flanked all the walls. Its clay floor would also be replaced by tile. The house now consisted only of a main room, a bedroom for Clay, and a kitchen. Later, according to his dreams, additions would be added. Rachel, the wife of Micah, had already planted morning glory, wisteria, and roses in the expectation they would climb the gallery poles and provide shade and coolness by the time the great heat of summer in South Texas arrived.

Nearby, the foundation and walls of the home Micah and Rachel would occupy had reached window level, with the empty frames of windows and doors rising skeletonlike against the sky. They lived now in a temporary structure beyond the main house. A saddleshop and blacksmith shop, also temporary, of chinked postoak poles stood down the slope near a holding corral that held four saddle horses. Half a dozen more horses were in sight in the bigger pasture along the creek. In the distance could be seen a few of the cattle that bore Clay's C-B brand. Southward, the land rolled onward to the wild country that led to wilder country in Mexico. A long day's ride in that direction lay the mysterious mountains of Coahuila which loomed above the horizon in pastel hues of mauve and burnt orange and pale violet. It was this that Clay Burnet had been laboring to imprison in paint on the oblong of canvas that had once been part of a chuck-wagon tarp. And failing, just as he had failed to capture contentment and peace in his heart.

Rachel's face appeared briefly over her husband's shoulder in the doorway. She was frightened. Little Lucinda peeked around her mother's skirt. Even at the age of six, Cindy was tuned to recognize the tensions and alarms of her elders, and to know the cause.

The Rangers had pretty well put a stop to the big raids. The Comanches rarely came down from the Llano Estacado in the numbers with which they had terrorized the Texas border during the war. Nor had the Apaches and the Kiowas been seen in more than a year in the San Dimas country.

Still, many of the young warriors had not given up. Small parties of Comanches from the north, Tonkaways from the refuge they had taken in Mexico, occasionally came through, hitting any settler's cabin they found off guard, but mainly bent only on stealing horses or butchering cattle.

"Tonk, maybe," Micah murmured. "I heerd talk when I was in Jackville a few days ago that some of 'em had crossed de rivah, accordin' to tracks thet was found."

They continued to wait, watching. Their hands suddenly tightened on the rifles. Then they lowered the weapons. Clay blew through his teeth in disbelief. Micah mumbled, "Oh, Lordy! It cain't be!"

A rider had emerged from the creek thickets. The horse evidently had been following the stream for safety's sake, for its belly dripped water. The arrival was a woman. She rode steadily up the slope toward the house, and pulled her mount to a stop at a few rods' distance.

She did not speak for a moment. She was a straight-backed woman well in her fifties, still handsome, with graying hair and fine gray eyes. She had a pistol in a saddle holster and a rifle in a scabbard. She rode sidesaddle in a riding habit. A straw sombrero was strapped to her head. Her mount was a broad-beamed, cat-quick cutting horse. A throw rope was coiled on the saddle.

"I came to talk," Rose Lansing said.

"About what?" Clay answered.

"About fools and feuds. About pride and conceit. About tombstones and weeping widows. About how it's time for the last of the Burnets and the last of the Lansings to act like human beings."

She continued to talk before Clay could frame his thoughts into words. "Don't say anything until you've heard me out. Oh, I know that I'm the first Lansing who ever set foot on your ranch, Clay Burnet. Just as—"

"Maybe not the first," Clay said.

"Lansings did not burn your ranch while you were at war," she said. "Indians did that. But no matter. That's in the past. I'm here, humbling my pride. No other Lansing has ever been in Burnet range to this day, just as you have never let your shadow touch anything claimed by the Lansings. I know about all the graves, and know who sleep in them, both Lansings and Burnets. I've wept for them, even for some of the Burnets, which you likely won't believe."

"You're right," Clay said. "I don't believe."

"And I don't give a hoot whether you believe or not. I said *some* of the Burnets. There were some that weren't worth a woman's tears."

"Even so, Burnet women wept for them," Clay said. "Now there's none left, even for weeping."

Rose Lansing made a hopeless gesture and touched her horse, starting to swing it to ride away. Then she halted. "No!" she said, throaty emotion in her voice. "No! I'm not going to go until I've been heard out. Even a Burnet should have sense enough to know I came in peace."

"Don't tell me you came alone?"

She waved that aside. "Listen to me, if you will, or stand on your foolish pride, if that pleases you, like all of the Burnets in the past."

She watched Clay's eyes search the brush of the creek. "There are no other Lansings there," she said. "I didn't come here to lure you into the open so that you could be shot. That's what's in your mind, isn't it?"

"Tonks are said to be in the country," Clay said. "They can shoot too and they'd like to get their hands on a woman. You know that."

"I'll make it as brief as possible," she said. "There's money to be made if men in this range will get off their tails and quit feeling sorry for themselves."

"I'm happy," Clay said.

Rose Lansing's eyes traveled over the surroundings. If she was aware of the evidence that this was only the beginning—the start of the restoration of the Burnet fortunes, she gave no sign. If she was thinking of the ashes that were all that had remained of the Burnet ranch house when Clay had returned from Appomattox a year in the past, her eyes remained stony. Clay believed the Lansings had destroyed his birthplace, thinking that none of the Burnets remained alive. They had been wrong. Clay had come back from the battlefields, where two of his brothers were in their graves.

Her gaze finally settled on the unfinished painting on the easel. She kneed her horse closer and took her time studying the canvas. She twisted around in the saddle to appraise the landscape that Clay had as his subject. She made no comment.

"Men can be happy, and still rot in their minds," she said. "Are you going to permit me to dismount? I've ridden quite a few miles today, and I'm not as young as I could wish."

Clay hesitated a moment, then moved to give her a hand

down. She accepted it, and smiled bitterly as she watched him absently scuff his palms together afterward.

"Children in my family were taught to feel that there was contamination in touching a Burnet," she said. "I see that you were brought up to feel the same way about Lansings."

"You mentioned that you had something to say," Clay said.

"I believe you already know what's in my mind. Talk travels fast in the San Dimas. Some men have nothing else to do."

"I've heard something," Clay admitted.

"Jem Rance, I imagine. He'd ride forty miles to spread news, twice that far if it wasn't true."

"He only had to ride forty this time, I take it," Clay said.

"Well, it's true. I've asked the San Dimas ranchers to forget their petty jealousies and everybody pool together in shaping up a herd to drive north to find a market."

"Who's everybody?"

"Myself, Jem Rance, Ike Turner, Jess Randall, Ham Marsh, Pete Fosdick, and some others."

"Others like Parson Jones and Beaverslide Smith?" Clay asked. "Or Uncle Cal Pryer? I understand they're considering it."

"Like they've been considering getting off their rears ever since the war, but never quite getting around to it. They'd rather sleep on the bank of a creek, waiting for a catfish to bite, or wait in a blind to pick off a deer while they let their wives and kids live in shacks, wear rags, and go barefoot. They seem to think the world ended when Lee gave up the ghost at Appomattox. They talk big and think small. They just dream."

"Or maybe waste their time daubing paint on canvas," Clay said.

She did not yield. "There's a time to dream and a time to work. We all own cattle, plenty of them. All they're

worth here in San Dimas is maybe four bits for their hides—
if we can find a hide buyer. But there's a market for beef
if we've got the gumption to take advantage of it."

"Just where would this market be?" Clay asked.

"There are places in Louisiana where cattle can be
shipped by steamboat up the Mississippi to big cities," she
said. "New Orleans, Shreveport. It's already been done."

"And the drovers came back broke, such as came back
alive," Clay said. "I fought in that country. At Vicksburg
and other places. Swamps, cypress jungles. And I've talked
to men who made cattle drives to the Mississippi last year.
They lost two thirds of their herds and the rest brought
only hide money, for they were down to skin and bones."

"Then there's Missouri," Rose Lansing said grimly. "Rail-
roads have built into Missouri, and into Kansas too, but
I expect Missouri is the closest."

"That's been tried also," Clay said. "Half a dozen herds
were shoved north last year. The most of them hit nothing
but misery. Storms, stampedes, Indians. A lot of 'em were
buried up there, and a lot of 'em came back afoot, busted."

"But some of them made money, good money. A man told
me that cattle would bring fifteen, maybe twenty dollars
a head at the railroad in Missouri. Do you know what that
kind of money would mean to us here in the San Dimas?"

"Trouble," Clay said. "And grief. Plenty of both."

"It would buy silk dresses for every wife in the San
Dimas."

"Black silk," Clay said. "Mourning dresses."

"And it might add twenty more years to their lives in
place of working themselves into their graves, peeling hides,
chopping cotton so as to put food in the mouths of their
children."

"We fought people like the ones you'll find in this
Missouri or Kansas," Clay said. "We won't be welcome. The
hatreds of war don't die easy. That country's full of outlaws, guerrillas, cutthroats."

"Colonel Pierce says it can be done. Fact is, he's done it."

"Colonel Pierce? Who's he?"

"They call him 'Shanghai' Pierce. He passed through here a few weeks ago. He's a cattleman from the coast. He's making money and has great plans for grading up cattle, for bringing in humpbacks from India. He says they'll thrive on the coast, for they resist ticks, fever. He's a man who doesn't believe in waiting for catfish to bite."

Clay had heard of "Shanghai" Pierce. He was impressed but refrained from admitting it. He swept his arms to encompass the scene around. "Money can't buy this," he said. "Did you ever really look at what we have here? Did you ever really see the coming of spring, see the colors in the Del Burros across the line? There's more to this world than cattle and money."

"Don't lecture me about beauty and peace," Rose Lansing said. "I was daubing away at trying to put all this on canvas when you were a wet-nosed brat, young man. I've had my dreams. I hunt for peace of mind too. But you can't live on dreams. Can't you see your future? Look around you. Look at men like Ham Marsh. Forty years old, and he looks sixty. All he does is move from place to place around the shack to let the sun warm him. He carries gossip instead of looking for something useful to do. Look at Pete Fosdick, at Nate Fuller, at *all* of them. I propose that we drive twenty-five hundred head of cattle to market. Think what that would do for these people—and for us."

Clay was staring at her. Her words, "I hunt for peace of mind too," kept echoing in his memory. Had that been an accidental figure of speech, or did she know about that day—that terrible day far from Texas at a place with the incongruous name of Hatcher's Run? The day Hatcher's Run had surged along as a red tide, the hue of soldier blood? Did she really know that the face of her son kept rising in his mind every day, almost every hour, tearing at his conscience, turning his dreams to nightmares, destroying his vista of the future? Did she know that he had ordered Phil Lansing to his death that awful day when the Yankees were driving relentlessly on the faltering men in gray?

"I'm happy here," he said. "I've got everything a man needs."

"Everything?"

Once more he suspected she was impaling him on the sharp point of her knowledge of that day. "You're still dreaming," he said. "Twenty-five hundred head of beef stock. It would take months to round up that many in the San Dimas."

"How many could you round up in two weeks' time?"

"I tell you I don't want any part of this!" he said.

"I happen to know that you don't sit here all the time smearing paint on that piece of canvas," she said. "You've been popping the brush for wild cattle ever since you got back from the war, branding young stuff, beefing mosshorns and barren cows for hides and tallow to earn a few dollars and cut down overgrazing. You've got a respectable start on a new herd. I would estimate that you could gather maybe two hundred head of good, strong fours and fives that could make it up the trail."

Clay was driven to boast a trifle. "More like three hundred if Micah and me put our minds to it. But that's a long way from twenty-five hundred."

"I can put around three hundred head into the pool from our Loop L," she said. "The other ranchers tell me they'll be able to get seven or eight hundred, maybe nine. They've all got some beef in their brands that are only growing horns and meanness."

"That still doesn't add up to twenty-five hundred."

"I've contracted with Pedro Sanchez across the river for a thousand head of prime cattle at four dollars a head. It's up to us to furnish the other fifteen hundred."

"That figures up to four thousand dollars for Pedro Sanchez," Clay said. "What are you going to use for money? This range is flat busted."

She ignored that. "He will deliver the cattle to our crew at the river on the fifteenth day of April. That's only three weeks away."

"Crew? What crew?"

"I've already named the most of them."

"You don't really mean—?"

"Why not? And who else? Ham Marsh, Beaverslide Smith, the Parson, Nate Fuller, Cal Pryer. They're men, aren't they?"

"You *are* dreaming," Clay said. "Parson Jones is past seventy if he's a day. Beaverslide is up in years too. Cal Pryer is maybe older than either of them. Ham Marsh is a tub of lard. He likely wouldn't last as far as the Brazos. He'd be afoot inside a week, for he's hell on horseflesh. Nate Fuller is too lazy to get out of his tracks. Some of them are moonshiners who drink their own rotgut. The lot of them haven't been too choosey about beefing cattle that wear other people's brands, including yours and mine. They steal horses, too, if the sign is right."

"It sounds like the makings of a good trail crew," she said.

"Lady, you don't know what you're talking about. The trail's rough, tough."

"Exactly. That's why we will need someone who knows how to handle a big outfit. You were an officer in the cavalry. They say Jeb Stuart considered you to be a top leader. You're to be trail boss."

"You must be out of your mind," Clay said. "And I'd be out of mine if I tried to handle a ragtag outfit like that."

"If these men are the weaklings you say they are, then they need a strong hand," she said. "The Burnets always posed as better than their betters. You're a Burnet."

"I'm telling you no," Clay said.

In the background Micah spoke softly. "Somethin' movin' ag'in in the shinnery."

Rose Lansing instantly moved close to the horse, using it as a shield, and dragged her rifle from the scabbard. She had lived through the days of the big Comanche and Kiowa raids. She had seen her husband die with a Tonkaway arrow through his lungs. The walls of the Loop L ranch house bore the scars of spears and fire arrows.

Clay moved to her side, also using the animal as a barrier. He crouched, scanning the creek brush from beneath the animal's belly. He saw movement in the thickets.

"Micah," he said. "Whatever is there is near that big bee tree. You can notch on it from the front window. Take my Henry and put a few slugs through the nest. Maybe that'll smoke 'em into the open."

The bee tree was a hollow oak that had been taken over by a swarm. He heard Micah hurry through the house. Then came the shots. He saw dust rise from the punky wood of the oak where the bullets had struck.

There was a moment of silence. Then a rider came bursting from the thickets. Not an Indian. Again the arrival was feminine. A young woman. She crouched low in the saddle, urging the horse to greater speed. She headed the animal up the slope toward the house. She was being pursued by a comet tail of bees.

"She's bringin' 'em down on us!" Micah shouted. "De Lawd's goin' to punish de just an' de unjust. Everybody into de house! Slam de doors! Shet dem windows!"

The girl and the bees arrived. Rose Lansing tossed the reins over her horse, slapped it on the rump and sent it galloping away. She raced for the nearby kitchen door which Rachel held wide for her.

Clay, taken aback, waited until the victim of his inspiration leaped from her horse in a running dismount. "You damned rascals!" she screamed, and raced for the door. Bees buzzed like bullets. Clay felt the hot-iron thrust of their anger on his neck. He and the girl tore through the doorway together with such haste their legs tangled and they landed in a heap on the rag rug that Rachel had plaited for the kitchen floor.

She placed boot heels against Clay's chest and violently parted herself from him. "What in blazes are you trying to do?" she raged. "Break my neck?"

"Kick me once more, and I might consider it," Clay gasped.

She scrambled to her feet. It had been four or five years since Clay had seen Ann Lansing at close range, and even then no Burnet or Lansing would let on that the other existed. She had been fifteen or sixteen, a lofty-nosed, leggy, shrill-voiced impossible person, who in Clay's opinion, needed to be turned over a knee and tanned in the right place. As far as he was concerned, all the Lansings had acted as if they were heirs of the earth and planets, and Ann Lansing, the youngest of the clan, had been the snootiest of the lot.

She was in her early twenties now and still unmarried. Who'd want a wife who wore jeans under a divided calico skirt, rode astride, rolled her own smokes and could handle a throw rope from the deck of a hard-mouthed bronco? It was said she could handle strong language, and Clay knew for a fact that she could stick in the saddle of a bucking horse about as long as any cowhand.

She was glaring witheringly at him with those Lansing eyes—gray-green, dominating. She swung a hand, knocking away a bee that was trapped in one of the buns of golden-bronze hair that she had plaited into two pigtails to fit under the weathered sombrero she had been wearing. She had skin tanned to the shade of fine chamois brown. She was slim and straight, her chin and mouth well-tooled— and aggressive.

She apparently had escaped the major wrath of the insects that still buzzed angrily around the walls of the beleaguered house. Not so, Clay. The bees had left fiery brands on his upper lip, a cheekbone, his forehead, and his hands. Rachel was already coming with homemade lotions to aid both of them.

He returned glare for glare with Ann Lansing as Rachel tended their hurts. "Only a Lansing," he said, addressing Micah, "would sneak up on a ranch like an Indian. Lucky we haven't got a dead one or two on our hands."

Ann Lansing acted as though he was not present. She spoke to her mother. "Mother!" she said severely. "What's come over you to be found at a place like this? Haven't you any pride?"

"You shouldn't have followed me, dear," Rose Lansing said. "There *could* be Indians around."

"It wasn't Indians I was worried about. It was you. Are you out of your mind, Mother?"

"It seems that you're not the only one who thinks so, dear. I was asked the same question only a few minutes ago. As a matter of fact, I feel that this is the most rational thought I've had in a long time."

"Rational? You call it rational to come here and humble yourself to this—this person? It's humiliating."

"I don't feel the least humiliated," Rose Lansing said. "I came here to—"

"Some of our people will be turning over in their graves," Ann Lansing said. "What would Father say, if—"

"If some of them had forgotten their stiff-backed pride, they might not be in their graves," Rose Lansing said crisply. "I came here to discuss a business matter with Clay Burnet."

"It's this beef-herd scheme that's on your mind. What has that to do with this—this person?"

"Burnet's the name," Clay said.

Ann Lansing continued to ignore him. "Bill Conners told me you might do something like this, Mother, and I've been watching you to prevent it. But you slipped away from me this morning."

Rose Lansing smiled fondly. "I told Bill to hide your saddle," she said. "I knew you were watching me. I see that you had your old hull hid out somewhere."

"Never mind what saddle I'm riding! We're heading back home right now, Mother. Hurry, before I get to feeling any more crawly than I do. I'll have to scrub to get the smell of this place off me."

"Spoken like a true Lansing," Clay said. "I didn't want to mention it, but I'm beginning to feel a little itchy myself."

"It's time to let bygones be bygones," Rose Lansing said. "The San Dimas should be a good country where men could lift their heads and live decently instead of having to turn to thievery. They need a man with iron in his backbone who would shame them into getting out of their ruts—or bulldoze them into it."

"I'm not much for bulldozing humans around," Clay said.

"You were an officer in the Texas Brigade," she said. "That's why I came here. You are the man, the only one, for this."

"That was another time, another world," Clay said. "That was war."

"You can't convince me you'd prefer to stay here and hide from life," she said.

Clay stiffened. "All I ask is to live in peace. I saw enough of the other kind."

"Peace is a state of mind," Rose Lansing said. "You can't buy it with wishes. You can't win it by trying to paint it."

"Come, Mother," Ann Lansing said. "Leave him to his daubing. Let him live in peace, and in poverty."

"I want him to boss the herd up the trail," Rose Lansing said.

"What? Him? Boss it? Why, they'd never—"

"They all know Mr. Burnet's war record," her mother said. "They would respect him, at least."

"But—but, he's a Burnet. He's a coward! He just as much as admitted it."

Rose Lansing ignored her daughter. "You can't refuse," she said.

"I am refusing," Clay said. "I've talked to men who've been up the trail. They go without sleep, without grub, without all the soft things of life. They drown in rivers that no man ought to ask them to risk. Indians kill them, torture them. Outlaws waylay them. I've had my share of ordering men to their deaths. I want no part of it."

"Some things are worse than dying," Rose Lansing said. "Think of Jem Rance and his children who've never owned enough shoes to go around, and of his wife who looks like an old woman when she's barely forty. Think of Parson Jones, trying to help grub out a living for half a dozen grandchildren, now that his three sons never came back from the war. And the rest of them. Ham Marsh, Beaverslide. Think of them when you're trying to paint this picture of beauty and peace."

She turned to Micah. "I think the bees are gone. If so, Micah, will you catch up our horses. We're leaving."

"Catch up the claybank for me, Micah," Clay said. "I'll be with you in a few minutes, ladies."

"With us? What do you mean?"

"I'll see you back to your place," Clay said. "I can't let females ride alone in this country—not even Lansings."

"That isn't necessary," Rose Lansing said.

"It certainly is not," her daughter sniffed.

"Rachel," Clay said. "Get my sidegun and shellbelt. See that there are a dozen shells in the loops, and fetch me a handful for the Henry. Where are my saddleboots?"

"I'd rather ride with a skunk," Ann Lansing said. "Stop acting like a tin hero. There are no Indians in the San Dimas, and you know it. Some people are always sending out scare stories. Those tracks somebody claims to have seen at the river likely were made by wild horses."

"I hope you're right," Clay said. "In that case I'm looking forward to being a tin hero. They're the kind that don't get killed. I've got no yearning to stop a slug, not to speak of an arrow or a spear. They all hurt. Then, again, you might be wrong. Even a skunk might be helpful if you ran into any copperskins between here and the Loop L."

Ann Lansing, finding she had no support from her mother, was forced to stand by, disdainful, but helpless while the preparations were made. When Micah brought up the horses, she helped her mother mount, a chore that was unnecessary, for Rose Lansing was supple and agile.

"Thet lady is might set in her ways," Micah murmured to Clay. "Brung up to hate the Burnets, an' keep the feud alive. Have you ever figured out what started thet feud, Claymore?"

Micah and Rachel were the only persons who ever addressed Clay by the full name that had been given him at birth. They had been free people from childhood, freed by Clay's father.

Clay shrugged. For the first time, it came to him that he really did not know the origin of that hatred between the clans.

CHAPTER 2

The Burnet-Lansing feud had its roots back in the hazy blue ridges of the Tennessee mountains before the Revolutionary War, when men wore coonskin caps and carried the long Kentucky rifles. That was more than a century in the past, and no man or woman seemed to know for certain what had started it. Clay's father had said he believed it had been something over a woman whose character had been assailed by the Lansings. The Lansings had it the other way and that it was one of their females who had been insulted. Clay had heard other stories, handed down from grandsires, that it had been something over the rights to a bear that had been felled by simultaneous shots from Burnet and Lansing rifles. Other stories had it that it began at a cabin-raising when young roosters from the Lansing and Burnet families had got into it, and it had ended in a shooting.

Whatever the forgotten cause, Burnets and Lansings had feuded and hated and dueled and slain in their native hills. It was the nature of the men of both families to be electrified by the saga of the Alamo in Texas's struggle for independence from Mexico. Unknown to each other, Burnet men and Lansing men had headed west to join in the Texan cause, with Davy Crockett as their martyred idol.

They had found Texas to their liking and had taken root there. Not until too late did the feuding families discover that once again they were neighbors. Perhaps it was because the hills of the San Dimas, the wilderness, the sense of independence and freedom in an untrampled land, was

reminiscent of the Tennessee country, that they found themselves confronting each other in their adopted land.

Even though there were no longer ambushes along dark
trails in laurel thickets, formal duels, and bitter hand-to-
hand conflicts, the feud had been kept traditionally alive.
Until now, no Lansing had crossed the deadline into Burnet
range. No Burnet had set foot on land claimed by a
Lansing. Rose Lansing was the first to break down the
barrier. There were no Lansing men left to protest this
defiance of family pride. Of the Burnets only Clay remained. The men of both families had hurried to the battlefields with the same ardor that had brought the clans west
to support Texas.

Clay remembered the kisses, the cheers, the kerchiefs that
had been tied to his sleeves and those of his brothers by
the women of Jackville, the thrill of it all, as they had
ridden away to war that bright day in '61. Company A,
San Dimas Volunteers, on their way to join the Texas
Brigade. Four Burnets. Clay, his father and two brothers.
And there had been three Lansings in the San Dimas contingent, two of Ann Lansing's brothers and an uncle. The
demands of war and discipline had brought the feuding
families into a common cause, but the old barrier existed.
No Burnet had shared bivouac or campfire with a Lansing,
no matter how harrowing had been the need for common
comradeship. The feud had endured through the terrors
of cannonfire and slaughtered humans.

Clay was the only one who had returned. During those
nightmare years he had learned a bitter truth. They had all
ridden off posing as crusaders, but the truth was that they
had feared the finger of scorn. No Burnet, no Lansing had
wanted to be branded as a coward.

The unyielding pride that had been the hallmark of the
two clans was exemplified in the rigid posture of Ann
Lansing. She urged her mount to a gallop as though she
wanted to put as much distance as possible between herself

and a Burnet. She was leading the way directly toward the creek brush from which she had come.

"Not so fast, dear!" her mother remonstrated, stirring her own horse into a lope in an attempt to keep pace.

Clay used spurs on his mount, lifting the surprised claybank into a full gallop. He swept past the mother and overtook the daughter. Before Ann Lansing realized his purpose he caught the bridle of her horse.

"Slowly, slowly," he said.

"Get your hands off my horse!" she snapped angrily. "What do you think you're doing?"

"It would be better if we crossed the pasture and forded the creek well beyond the brush there to the left," Clay said. He continued to keep control of her horse. She had a quirt on the saddle and she reached for it in a fury. Then she thought better of it.

"What do you mean?" she demanded. "That's a mile out of the way."

"But it will steer us clear of anyone who happened to have trailed you and your mother and is hunkered down there in the shinnery."

"You're only trying to be dramatic," she said. "And you're only succeeding in acting like a fool. Like a Burnet."

"Maybe you don't think it's worth while to ride a mile out of the way to save your scalp, but I don't mind," Clay said.

Ann Lansing saw that she was again in the minority. Her mother had arrived and was obviously in agreement with Clay. "It's a waste of time," she said. She had been defeated this time, but there was no yielding in her otherwise.

Clay scanned the brush, which stood well to their right as they circled through open fields and crossed the stream. There was no sign of danger. If Ann Lansing found any vindication in this, she refrained from taking advantage of it. She continued to ride in silence at her mother's side.

Rose Lansing, evidently fearing that her daughter would refuse to follow if Clay took the lead, moved ahead and began picking out their route. She was accepting Clay's viewpoint that caution took precedence over pride, and was steering clear of broken ground and thickets that might offer cover to a foe. This added considerable distance to the ride. Even so, it was not always possible to stay clear of possible trouble, for these Rincón Hills were rugged and broken, clothed with scrub live oak or the inevitable tough, thorny growth of South Texas. The brush grew tall and heavy in the pockets of the draws that they were forced to cross, for seeps of moisture lingered there.

Clay's C-B spread was lost to sight in the tangle of hills back of them as they made their way eastward. The late sun was mild on the back of his neck. He rode with his rifle in his hands, for he had an uneasy sensation of danger. He had known that same harsh touch of fear in the past on battlefields. Here, there was nothing to explain it. The Rincóns dozed dreamily around him. Invisible fingers of breeze gently stirred the tufts of new grass and brought to life the brush in the swales.

A few cattle faded off into the land in the distance as they advanced. Some bore his brand, no doubt. Others might be neighbors' cattle, even belonging to the Lansings. Others could be mavericks. The country was full of cattle, some branded, but the majority at the disposal of any brush popper who wanted to take the trouble of roping them, building a fire to burn his mark into their hides, and cropping an ear. For the majority of the San Dimas settlers the game was not worth the trouble. There were often broken legs, arms, ribs and dead horses on the debit side of the ledger. And broken necks. Brush popping was a hazardous way of earning hide money. The only reward was a man's pride in himself. Clay and Micah had popped the brush. They had built up a respectable brand in the year they had worked together since the war.

Clay looked ahead and drew a breath of satisfaction. They were emerging from the Rincón Hills, which was regarded as Burnet range, and descending into an open flat. Safer country. Half a dozen miles away rose other low hills. These were the Lagunas—Lansing country.

As they advanced into the flat he relaxed still more, feeling that any danger, if there had been danger, was over. He was wrong. Rose Lansing uttered a wild scream of warning. Her daughter echoed it with fear. Clay saw the cause also—too late. He saw the flash of the arrow in the late sun an instant before it tore through the latigo leather on his saddle and buried itself in the calf of his leg.

He saw the Indian who had loosed the arrow. The warrior had been forced to stand erect in the small gully in which he had been waiting in ambush. He was a Tonkaway. A bullet struck him before he could fix another shaft to his bow. Rose Lansing had fired. The force of the slug knocked the Tonkaway down, but other Indians were there and arrows were coming. The horses were pitching wildly, and the shafts missed.

Clay felt the shock of his wound. He forced himself to ignore that, and came into action with his rifle. Rose Lansing's weapon was a single shot Springfield, but his Henry was a shock to the warriors. They leaped into view after he had fired once, expecting to race to hand-to-hand combat with quarry whose weapons were empty. They wanted the women alive. Clay downed their leader, who wore the single feather of a chief. He wounded another. There had been five in all in the charge, and the survivors raced back to cover again, dragging the wounded with them.

The horses carried Clay and the two women out of range. A few more arrows were loosed, but fell short. Then they were safe, letting the animals run at full gallop. They crossed a swale, tore through thin brush, and emerged once more into open flats.

Clay brought his claybank down to a walk. "Easy, easy!" he called to the women. "Your hair is safe this time. Lucky they seemed to be afoot."

Mother and daughter were pale, but maintaining taut composure. That was the Lansing code. Rose Lansing spoke. "We'll go on to the ranch and send word to Dan King. They'll soon run those rascals down."

Dan King was Ranger captain, in charge of the San Dimas area, with headquarters in Jackville, which was the county seat.

Ann Lansing said nothing. She rode poker-faced, still refusing to acknowledge Clay's presence. He had been right about taking precaution against ambush, and she had been wrong. It was a dubious triumph over her, for his injury was taking toll, and he was in no mood to drive the harpoon deeper.

The stabbing pain suddenly nauseated him. He pulled his horse to a stop and slid from the saddle. The arrow was a hideous, snakelike length that clung to his flesh. Its head had driven entirely through the muscles of his calf and had emerged into the clear. He felt blood in his boot.

Until this moment the Lansings had not realized that he had been hit. They pulled up their horses. The mother uttered a small cry of dismay and swung from the saddle. She ran to his side. "Why didn't you tell us?" she cried. Clay feared she was going to faint.

He caught her by the shoulders, shaking her. "Get some sand in your craw, ma'am!" he said. "If there's one thing we can do without right now, it's a swooning woman. Get a bandage ready. That scarf around your daughter's neck will do. I'm going to pull this damned thing out of my leg now. I'll drip some, but I'm not going to die. It's only through the meat and not deep."

Ann Lansing had dismounted also. Her lips were the color of a tombstone, her cheeks hollow and ghastly. Like her mother, she was fighting off faintness.

"The neckerchief, the neckerchief!" Clay snapped. "Don't stand there gawking. If you expect me to beller, you're going to be disappointed. Give me that neckerchief, or do I have to take it off your gullet myself?"

Ann Lansing removed her neckerchief. It was of Mexican make, and of silk, yellow and blue, with a serpent design threaded through its center. Her fingers were quivering.

Her mother took the cloth. "I'll handle this," she said. She had fought off the faintness. She looked around, then took Clay by the arm and led him to a boulder on which he could sit. She knelt before him. "Knife?" she asked. "I've got to cut away your boot."

"On my horse," he said. "In the saddle pocket on this side."

Ann Lansing brought his skinning knife, and the mother slit his trousers and the boot. Blood flowed freely when she removed the boot. She formed a tourniquet with the neckerchief and used the knife as a lever to increase tightness.

Clay broke off the head of the arrow and drew the shaft from the wound. Pain became a searing flood, and the scene swam crazily before his eyes. That eased, and he looked sheepishly at Rose Lansing. "It did make me wince a little," he admitted. "Lucky it wasn't a war arrow. It was only a small one. They must have been out for meat—rabbits or prairie dogs—and happened to sight us."

Rose Lansing could not answer. She was sharing with him the pain. So was her daughter. "What—what if—if it was poisoned?" Ann Lansing mumbled.

"If so I'd know it by now," Clay said. "That stuff the Tonks use works *muy pronto*, and for keeps, so they say. That's one worry off my mind. Now, if you'll move that bandage down over that scratch I'd appreciate it. I got blood that thickens in a hurry. I'll likely be as good as new by sunrise."

Dazed Rose Lansing complied. Clay arose and moved

toward his horse. "Sorry I ruined your pretty scarf," he said to Ann Lansing as he pulled himself into the saddle.

"Hold on!" Rose Lansing cried. "What in the world? Where are you going?"

"Back home," Clay said. "You two will be all right from here on. In another mile you'll be in sight of your place."

"You'll do nothing of the kind," she said. "You're going with us to our house so that we can take proper care of that wound."

"Rachel will look after it," Clay said. "She's doctored a lot worse than this scratch."

Rose Lansing was angry. "I'm sure I can do anything Rachel Stone can do. You're being a fool, and you know it. It's ten miles to your place and those Tonks can still be hanging around in the Rincóns. Don't try to be so infernally tough. That leg needs attention. It needs more than that piece of silk. It needs a doctor. Do you want to lose your leg? We can have Horace Peters out from Jackville hours sooner than he could make it to your ranch."

Ann Lansing decided the issue. She swung aboard her horse, moved in, plucked the reins of Clay's mount from his hands, and said, "Come, Mother. Haven't you learned that it's only a waste of time talking to mules or Burnets. They have to be driven."

Clay tried to regain control of the situation—and of his horse. He failed. He tried to glare Ann Lansing into submission, but discovered that there were two or three Ann Lansings gazing haughtily at him. They began to whirl crazily around him.

He heard Rose Lansing cry out, "Ann! Grab him! He's falling!"

He felt arms around him, steadying him in the saddle. His head cleared a trifle, and he found himself peering uncertainly into the eyes of Ann Lansing at very close range.

He tried to retreat to safer distance. "I don't want to be

beholden to any damned, high-nosed Lansing," he found himself mumbling.

But she continued to hold him in the saddle. They rode in this position until they reached a trickle of water that bubbled along a small gully. Water was dashed into his face. That cleared his head somewhat. He suffered the humiliation of being helped to the ground by feminine hands.

"Ride to the ranch and fetch the men and the spring wagon, Ann," Rose Lansing said. "And send someone to town to bring Horace Peters. We'll be all right here for a while."

CHAPTER 3

Clay came entirely back to reality. "I'm all right," he mumbled. "I sort of went wa-wa, I'm afraid. I was thinking I was in the field hospital at Petersburg, and . . ."

He quit talking, shocked. He realized he must still be a trifle wa-wa. He hadn't meant to mention the war, particularly to a Lansing and to Rose Lansing, above all. And Petersburg, above all. Petersburg had been the pivotal point in the major battle of which Hatcher's Run had been a small part. Clay still bore the scars of the shellburst that had sent him to the field hospital after Hatcher's Run.

Rose Lansing was gazing at him, and in her face was a pitiful hope that he would keep talking. He turned his head away, refusing to comply with that unspoken demand. She drew a sighing breath, then busied herself with the bandaging. "I'll have to use part of your shirt," she said, and Clay heard the knife ripping away at cloth.

Ann Lansing had been listening, and in her was the same demand that tore at her mother. When Clay did not speak, she mounted and headed away toward the Laguna hills, in which the Lansing headquarters stood.

Rose Lansing said nothing more until she had finished applying a firm bandage. "Then you were at Petersburg?" she finally said, trying to make the question appear casual. "That is a place in Virginia where a terrible battle was fought in the last months of the war. My last letter from my son mentioned Petersburg. I—we never heard from him again. He is listed as missing in action, but—but we don't know how or where he fell."

Clay dreaded the next question. Rose Lansing knew Clay had been Phil Lansing's superior officer, knew that he must have been in the Hatcher's Run fight. She wanted to know how her son had died. Her lips formed the question, but the words did not come. She did not dare, for she seemed to fear the answer. Perhaps it was intuition, but she seemed to sense there was a dark shadow over Clay's knowledge.

She turned away. The situation that neither of them wanted to face was over for the moment at least. But Clay knew it would arise again, unless he was able to stay away from the Lansings. He tried to get to his feet with the intention of again mounting his horse. Rose Lansing pushed him back. "Wait for the wagon," she said. "You'll start the bleeding again. Do you want to die?"

"Quit treating me like a baby," he said. But he knew she was right. His attempt to move had offset the good effects of the fresh bandage. Rose Lansing had to cut more strips from his shirt to repair the damage.

He lay there expecting her to ask him again if he knew how Phil Lansing had died. He kept remembering how Phil Lansing's accusing, bitter eyes had kept looking out at him from his dreams, and from the darkness of the nights during all these months when peace of mind had evaded him. It was these visions that had robbed him of the tranquillity, the forgetfulness that he had sought here in the San Dimas—a thousand miles from Hatcher's Run.

Rose Lansing remained silent. She brought the horses closer at hand, tethering them to brush, then moved about on foot, rifle in hand, scanning the surroundings. Clay kept watch also, for there was always the chance the Tonkaways might have followed them, and could be creeping up on them.

Finally she spoke. "All right. The boys are in sight with the wagon."

The vehicle presently arrived. It was a long-reach, weathered old ranch wagon with a team of mules in harness, and driven by Dad Hoskins, an ancient cowhand who had been with the Lansings for many years. It was accompanied by Ann Lansing and the ranch foreman, Bill Conners. Conners was a bulky, muscular man, given to boasting of his strength and past exploits as a bare-knuckle boxer. He had served in the Rangers during the war, guarding against Comanche raids, and had been made foreman of the Loop L by Rose Lansing when the major conflict had ended.

The two men lifted Clay into the bed of the wagon on which blankets had been placed. "Easy, easy!" Clay remonstrated. "You're not bulldogging a maverick, you know."

"Too bad it wasn't your gullet that got stuck," Bill Conners said. "Then you wouldn't be able to beller like a branded calf—or like a Burnet."

Ann Lansing and Dad Hoskins laughed. Rose Lansing spoke. "That's enough of that. Now take it easy with that wagon, Dad. Walk the mules. If I see you trying any rough riding I'll drive the wagon myself. We don't want a dead man on our hands."

Even so, it was a rough ride to the Lansing ranch, but Clay refused to give Conners and Ann Lansing the satisfaction of complaining, even though Dad Hoskins failed to veer the mules away from some of the rough going. However, he was able to lift his head and peer with some interest when Lansing Manor finally came in sight.

Joseph Lansing had started it as a small adobe house to which additions had been added through the years—rockwalled wings, gabled frame structures, leantos—all connected by dogtrots or galleries until they formed a mansion that had somehow attained grandeur and dignity.

At a distance were quarters for servants and for the field hands who had once raised the crops that had fed the Lansings and their guests and the hay for their fine horses. Like the Burnets, the Lansings had never owned a slave. Free people themselves, the Lansings had believed in free-

dom for all. Also like the Burnets, they had gone to war
because of loyalty to their adopted state.

Now Lansing Manor was a skeleton of its past glory. Decay
had set in with the death of Joseph Lansing. Rose Lansing
had fought a losing battle against Indians, against rustlers,
against *bandidos* from across the river. The most damaging
factor had been lack of market for cattle. The quarters for
the field hands were now delapidated, with windows staring like toothless mouths, doors boarded shut. Only a small
portion of the rambling bunkhouse was used.

The main house was forlorn. Apparently only the west
wing was occupied. A few saddlemounts were held in the
corral that had contained scores in the past. A lone, ancient
foxhound came to challenge them, arising from the shade
of the gallery. The Lansings had once maintained a fine
pack of fox- and greyhounds for the pleasure of their guests
at hunting parties.

Clay let his head fall back. He had the guilty sensation
of having intruded into the chamber of the dying, of having
committed sacrilege. A dreary emptiness gripped him. On
him was the complete realization of the futility of it all, of
the price of war, and of the toll of mistaken pride.

Rose Lansing was looking at him and must have been
attuned to his thoughts. "Better that it had all been destroyed as your hacienda was destroyed," she said. "At least
you have the advantage of starting anew again as your
people did when they first came to the San Dimas. At
least you don't have to live with ghosts that jibber at you
from every doorway, from every window, every room."

"Mother!" Ann Lansing exclaimed. "Not now, please. And
not in front of—of people!"

A venerable, bald-pated black man, with a fringe of white
beard under his chin, came on rheumy legs to help, and
was sent by Rose Lansing to fetch a stretcher. Ben Tibbs
had been majordomo at the manor for years.

Clay, despite his protests that he could walk alone, was

carried into the manor and down a long hall. He had a
glimpse of wide, double doors of oak on which gilt paint
was fading. These, he surmised, must open into the salon,
as the Lansings had preferred to call the ballroom.

He was placed on cool sheets in a great wide canopied
bed in a room whose windows were set in adobe walls a
yard thick. A crèche in carved dark wood broke the blank-
ness of one wall, and a great crucifix and chain, also carried
from the same wood, was fixed to another. This, Clay
realized, must have been the guest room in which famous
personages had been entertained in the past.

Now Clay Burnet, the first of his clan ever to enter
inside these thick walls, lay on fine linen in the remnants of
his cotton shirt and worn saddle breeches, with the blood
of his bandages staining the finery.

A vigorous, middle-aged black woman with fine features
and a melodious voice took charge. Jenny Pleasant was the
widowed daughter of Ben Tibbs. Between them, they kept
the sinking pride of the Lansing clan alive.

"You git out of here, Anna Manana," Jenny Pleasant said,
stabbing a forefinger in Ann Lansing's direction. "This ain't
no place fer a young lady. I kin take care o' this hunk of
person. I'll fix him up, even if he is one o' dem dratted
Burnets."

"Anna Manana" meekly obeyed. "Is someone on the way
to Jackville to fetch Horace?" Rose Lansing asked.

"Yep, I sent Luke," Jenny sniffed. "But, from de looks,
it's a waste o' Mr. Peters' time. I kin do anythin' a doctah
kin do. This heah man ain't hurt bad."

"That's what I'm trying to tell everybody," Clay said,
attempting to get off the bed.

Jenny pushed him back. "You ain't *thet* perky," she said.
"Now you jest lay there 'til I tell you that you kin git up.
You hear me, Burnet man?"

Clay sank back. As a matter of fact he was glad to have
an excuse to give in to the authority of the black woman.

Jenny Pleasant removed the bandage from his leg and examined the wound. "You sure did git yoreself puncturated, didn't you?" she commented. "But you is lucky, like all you dratted Burnets. It missed de bone, else you might have had real trouble. But I got some salve dat will make you feel pretty frisky by tomorrow."

She applied medication and a fresh bandage. Then she brought a cooling lotion from the springhouse. It was a squeeze of berry juice, and it did wonders for his parched throat. The pain eased. Darkness came, and lamps were burning. He felt drowsy. He tried to fight that off, tried to get out of the bed.

It was Rose Lansing who held him back. He had not realized that she had been watching over him. "You must lie still," she said. "The doctor will soon be here."

"I don't need a doctor," he mumbled. "I need my horse— and a shirt. I can't ride home without a shirt at night. Mosquitos would eat me alive."

"And Tonkaways," she said. "You're staying here for the night at least."

"Micah will have fits if I don't show up at home."

"We've already sent word that you're here. He will come tomorrow to go back with you."

He realized that something had been put in the sweet drink. He surrendered to the drowsiness and slept. He was vaguely aware some time during the night that Horace Peters, the Range doctor from Jackville, was examining his wound.

He heard the crusty old doctor snort with disdain. "This fellow will be back on his feet in a hurry, Rosemary," Horace was saying. "He might be limping around for a while, but that's about all. You can't kill a Burnet that easy. You got me into a ten-mile trip for nothing, and furthermore, luck was running my way in the stud game at Hank's when I had to cash in. This will cost you about four fingers

of whisky—good whisky—as a starter. None of that forty-rod
heat lightning that Ham Marsh stills."

Clay drifted off again into sleep. He awakened to find
the sun streaming through the windows. His leg was offering no pain. Whatever cure-all Jenny Pleasant had used,
had been effective, evidently. Jenny came bustling in, bearing a tray that was loaded with a solid array of breakfast
items.

"Good mornin', Burnet man," she said. "I declare, I was
beginnin' to think you was goin' to be lazy all day. It's
goin' onto ten o'clock. Don't you never git any sleep over at
yore place? I fetched a considerable load of grub, figurin'
that, as you didn't git any suppah last night, you'd be in the
market for some fancy eatin'. Aftah you fill up I reckon you
kin git dressed. Yore clothes are on that chair. We rounded
up a shirt and boots that ought to fit you."

Clay dressed first, then ate. He ate heartily, even though
he had imagined in the past that his throat would revolt
against Lansing food.

He was sitting in a chair, finishing his coffee when Rose
Lansing tapped on the opened door, then entered. "I see
you are feeling better," she said. "Horace Peters is still here
and says there's nothing he can do that Rachel Stone can't
take care of without trouble. I'm afraid I won't get rid of
him until that bottle of liquor I've been saving for medic-
inal purposes is all gone."

Clay was listening to voices. He arose and hopped to
a window that overlooked the ranch yard. Half a dozen
men, some saddleback, others in harness rigs, were arriving
and being greeted as they alighted by other men who had
arisen from chairs on the gallery, evidently having pulled in
earlier. Stone jugs appeared and were passed around.

Clay knew them all—Jess Randall, Parson Ezra Jones,
Ham Marsh, Beaverslide Smith, Uncle Pryer, among others.
They were all San Dimas settlers. Some must have traveled

a considerable distance to attend this gathering. Nate Fuller, for one, lived on Big Turkey Creek, some forty miles north.

"What's going on?" Clay demanded of Rose Lansing.

"Just a powwow among neighbors," she said.

"It's about this scheme of yours to put a herd on the trail, isn't it?"

"Why don't you go out there and ask them about it?"

"Not interested," Clay said.

"At least you could talk it over."

"You can't really be serious, ma'am," Clay said. "Look at 'em! Look, I say! Old men, beaten men. Patched saddles, patched shirts, patched britches. How long do you figure they'd last on the trail?"

She went to a window and called to the arrivals. "I'll be right out. I'm bringing a neighbor with me."

"I'm not going out there," Clay hissed angrily. "I told you I don't want to—"

"To have to tell them what you just told me? Afraid to tell Beaverslide and Nate Fuller to their faces that they're no longer worth a hoot, and that they drink a quart of rotgut whisky a day? Afraid to tell Pete Fosdick and Parson Jones they'd fade out before they got to the Brazos?"

"That's not fair. I said—"

Her daughter was standing in the doorway, listening. There was a twisted smile on her lips. "Go ahead," she said. "Go on out there and tell them how much superior you are to them. Tell them they're a bunch of failures."

"No," her mother said. "It's not that at all. What we're actually saying is that these men haven't a chance to better themselves. What Mr. Burnet will have to tell them is that they might as well resign themselves to sinking deeper into despair, that their future is in the past, and that if they want to know what's ahead of them they only need to look back at yesterday—or to this morning."

"Better that than to be in their graves far from home,"

Clay said. "I've got ghosts enough on my back, without that."

Again that had been a slip of the tongue. For again, Rose Lansing was gazing at him, that wild question on her lips, the question she was again afraid to ask.

Using a chair as a crutch, Clay hobbled to the doorway. Ann Lansing stood for a moment as though deciding to block his way, then thought better of it and moved aside.

"Wait!" Rose Lansing cried. "I'll help you!"

Clay kept going. Using the walls of the hallway for support, he hopped and stumbled through the outer door onto the open gallery. The arrivals craned their necks, gazing in amazement. The Burnet-Lansing feud was the great legend of the San Dimas country. Every man, every woman and child knew the story and treasured it as a perpetual source of yarns and speculations that relieved a drab existence.

Clay saw his claybank horse in the holding corral, his saddle and headstall slung on a gear tree. He singled out Bill Conners. "I'd like my horse, Conners," he said. "And I'll need my sidearm and rifle."

Conners looked at Rose Lansing. She and her daughter had followed Clay to the gallery. The elder woman made a gesture of failure. Conners, with a shrug, nodded to Dad Hoskins, who left the group, hurried to the corral and caught up Clay's mount. Saddling it, he brought it to the gallery step. It was all done in silence as the San Dimas ranchers stared still not believing they were actually seeing a Burnet on Lansing property.

Clay was handed his weapons. None offered help as he dragged himself aboard the horse and arranged his injured leg as comfortably as possible. Ann Lansing was the only one who moved. She came to stand at his stirrup, holding a yellow ribbon in her hand. "This is for you," she said, tying the ribbon to the bridle of Clay's mount.

Nobody spoke. The jugs of liquor that had been passing from hand to hand were motionless. During the war it had been the custom of Southern women to pin yellow ribbons on men they considered cowards.

Clay plucked the ribbon from its place and fixed it around his wrist. "Somebody might get the wrong idea that it was the horse and not me that you had in mind," he said.

He swung the claybank around and started to ride away. But Parson Ezra Jones stood in his path, forcing him to pull up. The Parson was a weather-blown oak of a man, craggy and knotty, with whitening hair, a hooked nose, and fierce eyes.

"Don't never mind what Miss Ann thinks, Clay," he said in his sonorous preaching voice. "We all know that you fought through the war, brave an' honorable. We are all hopin' you'll throw in with us. Rosemary Lansing has been proddin' an' pushin' us for weeks, so that we've begun to believe what she says. We're askin' you to forgit the past, forgit what you hold ag'in other folks. I know that me an' the others don't look like much to ride the trail with, but with the Lord's help, we'll git through somehow, for the sake of our womenfolk an' our children. We're askin' you to gamble three, four months o' your time and a few head o' cattle that ain't worth anythin' to you down here in the thickets. The rest of us are a riskin' a leetle more than that. We're throwin' everything into the pot."

"What's everything?"

"Our Range rights. The roofs over our haids. Some of our holdin's don't amount to much, but it's all we got. An' the Loop L is all Rosemary's got."

"I don't savvy."

"You can't buy a thousand head of Spanish reds on promises," the Parson said. "Such of us are throwin' into the pool have borrowed on what little we own, an' put it in with what Rosemary raised by mortgagin' the Loop L. Them bankers in San'tone shore drive hard bargains. All they'd loan me was four hundred dollars, even though a got a nice stretch of water frontage on Clear Crick. At one an' a half per cent interest a month. The rest o' the boys didn't do no better. Nor Rosemary either. Fifteen hundred dollars on the whole danged Loop L, lock stock an' barrel. Even in these days it's worth plenty more than that. We're all goin' for broke. Missouri or bust."

Clay glared accusingly at Rose Lansing. "So you talked them into this gamble," he said.

He kneed his horse into motion and rode past the silent group of San Dimas men, heading out of the ranch yard. After a moment he halted the animal. He sat fighting it out with himself for a space. Slowly he swung his mount around and returned. He slid from the saddle, sparing his bandaged leg as best he could.

Beaverslide Smith was holding one of the jugs that contained the white lightning that had been passing around. Pete Fosdick had just placed a second jug on the ground after imbibing. Clay drew his six-shooter and fired twice. The reports kettled all the horses within hearing. Broken pottery tinkled. The pungent fumes of spilled liquor drifted in the air. Pete Fosdick and Beaverslide stared unbelievingly at the remnants of the jugs.

"I can raise a little cash to sweeten the pot," Clay said. "From now on there'll be a time for work and a time for drinking. I'll be the one to decide when and where for each. Right now we've got to round up about fifteen hundred head of beef to add to that bunch of reds. I doubt if it can be done. I figure I can get together up to three hundred head, and Mrs. Lansing says she can do the same. What about you boys?"

They stood in amazed silence for a space. Then the Parson spoke, "I promise a hundred, maybe a few more."

A babble of voices arose as others estimated the numbers they could gather that would be fit for the trail.

"Unless it's just moonshine talk we might wind up with closer to three thousand head," Clay said. "As I understand it, we're to take delivery of the reds in three weeks at the river."

"But did you have to waste good likker thetaway?"
Beaverslide said mournfully.

Clay looked at Rose Lansing. Her eyes were alight. She
seemed younger. But her daughter stood straight and stiff-
lipped, and still hostile.

Micah did the hard riding in the brush and coulees of
the Rincóns, bringing in cattle that measured up to Clay's
standards. The majority were steers, along with a sprinkling
of strong, barren cows, all between the ages of four and six.
Rachel helped her husband, for she was a fine rider, and
with amazing endurance. She brought in her share of animals from the hills.

Clay, fuming at his helplessness, could do little more
than the cooking, entertain little Cindy, and ride guard on
the cattle that Micah and Rachel turned into the horse
pasture where the animals were content to partake of the
rich grazing.

By the fourth day his leg had mended so that he was able
to trade places with Rachel, an arrangement that pleased
everyone but Cindy, who preferred Clay's indulgence to
her mother's discipline.

"Thet's about it," Micah said days later. "You suah hit it
about right, Claymore. I tally 'em at two hundred an'
ninety odd. We've skimmed the cream an' a little more.
Some o' them fours might not be what I'd pay money for."

"They'll all do," Clay said. "They'll fatten some, believe it
or not, after we cross the Brazos, provided they have a smart
trail boss who knows how to handle cattle. They tell me
that grass will be stirrup high by the time we get there,
and I've heard that the Nations beyond Red River is a
paradise for cattle."

"These here Nations?" Micah asked uneasily. "Thet's a
regular hornets' nest o' Injuns, so I understand."

"We might see a few," Clay said. "We'll give them a
crippled steer or two and they'll let us alone."

"I shoah hope you ain't lyin' too much," Rachel spoke. "I don't want no truck with them no'thern redskins. They're meaner'n the ones we got down heah."

"Me neither," Cindy spoke. She was skipping a rope and playing hopscotch at the same time.

"Don't worry about Indians, Rachel," Clay said. "It's the gals in Missouri that Micah will have to fight off."

"I'll take care of that part o' the fightin'," Rachel said. "An' Cindy will help me. Any o' them black no'thern gals that makes eyes at my man will git them eyes damaged somewhat."

"Wait a minute!" Clay exclaimed. "You don't have any notion that you and Cindy are going along with the drive, do you, Rachel?"

"I am goin'," Rachel said. "An' I cain't leave Cindy here. I agreed it all with Missus Lansin' the other day when she rode over heah to see how things' was goin'. I'm to help her with the cookin', an' such, an' drive the bedwagon. My brotha, who lives in Jackville, is goin' to come out here an' look after this place. He's married an' reliable."

"Did I hear you right? You don't mean to say that Rose Lansing is thinking of going along with the drive too?"

"Dat's kerrect," Rachel said complacently. "Us ladies ain't got any notions of bein' left behind to fret an' worry about what mischief you men folk air gittin' yorselves into way up there. We figger we'll be needed."

"God help me!" Clay said.

"Miss Ann is goin' too," Rachel said. "I reckon that won't please you none either. She ain't got no more use fer you than a houn' dog fer a porkypine. I reckon she's goin' along to keep an eye on you."

Clay hurled his hat on the ground. "May the good Lord have mercy on me!" he frothed.

"I'm mighty happy to see that you're finally gittin' religion," Rachel said.

CHAPTER 4

Clay sat on his horse, looking at the river. The Rio Bravo, some called it. To the Mexicans it was the Rio del Norte, River of the North. Texans in this part of the world merely referred to it as the river. The Rio Grande's birthplace was in the high mountains of New Mexico, far away. Here, on the Mexico border, it bore the brown face of maturity and experience. It divided two nations. Armies had crossed and recrossed it. Outlaws from both sides used it to flee to sanctuary. Rustlers loved it. Cowboys feared it.

Clay was viewing a famous fording place that had been used since the days of the conquistadors. Here the river quieted, broadened to half a mile and offered fairly safe passage, especially in late summer. But this was spring. The river was rising. It had power. He could see the evidence of heavy current in the mid-stretches, a current that likely had gouged out deep holes that would offer the threat of savage undertows and strong eddies.

Around him were the men of the Patchsaddle drive. A dozen in all. A nondescript assembly. Jess Randall and Ike Turner still wore the infantry forage caps and ragged gray shirts in which they had returned after the surrender. Pete Fosdick had on a blue woolen shirt, faded by many washings, that looked suspiciously like one stolen from the Yankee garrison that had been stationed briefly at Jackville the previous summer. Among the others were patched cotton shirts, buckskin breeches, boots, and hats that had seen sad service.

In the background stood the chuck wagon and the canvas-hooded supply wagon. Rose Lansing in cotton dress, straw sombrero, and gauntlets sat on the seat of the chuck wagon, the reins of the four-mule team wrapped around the brake handle while she waited. Rachel and Cindy were on the seat of the supply wagon, in bright calico, and with bandanas around their heads.

Ann Lansing, mounted astride in breeches, leather chaps, flannel shirt, and brush jacket, sat with the men of the crew. During the work of assembling a thousand head of cattle, which were being held a day's ride north of the river, she had popped brush, hazed cattle, roped refractory animals, and had held up her end of the work in the thickets where even the horses wore bullhide breast-shields to protect them from the thorned cactus and mesquite.

At first, the presence of a trouser-wearing female had offended the old-timers, and also Clay. Now, even Clay had to admit grudgingly that it had been the only sensible thing to do. The other men now accepted her as though she was only another cowhand. Only young Lonnie Randall, the son of Jess Randall, seemed to remember that she was a comely young woman. Lonnie, sixteen years of age, was moon-eyed and love-smitten. A gangly, freckled, placid-natured youth, who was all elbows, knees, and Adam's apple, he managed to stay as close to her as possible whenever his duties as horse jingler with the *remuda* permitted. He was always eager to scramble hurriedly to anticipate her wants.

Clay gazed beyond the far shore of the river. Two riders were approaching the stream from the south. Both wore steeple-crowned sombreros. One was mounted on a saddle whose silver trim caught the glint of the sun. The other was evidently a leathery *vaquero*.

Clay lifted an arm and raised his voice to the utmost. "*Buenos días, Señor Pedro!* We are ready!"

On the flats beyond the river he could see the brown scatter of cattle that were being held on grazing by more *vaqueros*.

The Mexican ranchero answered with a beckoning arm, but what words he uttered were carried away by the wind.

Clay looked at his crew. "All right," he said. "He's got the cattle. Let's cross."

His glance traveled from face to face. He saw them appraising the river. They knew the Rio Grande, knew it very well. He waited for the fear to show, for some to shrink. None did.

It was Beaverslide Smith who spoke. "Come on, you brand-pickers. Shake a laig. The quicker we git them Mex cows acrost to God's country the better. Thet river's raisin', an' raisin' fast."

Next to the elderly Parson Jones, Beaverslide was the one Clay had picked to cave in the earliest. But it was the old bald-headed cowman who now led the Patchsaddle crew into the river. He led with a whoop and slap of his hat on the rump of his horse. The others, yelling also, joined him. Spray flew, horses kicked up sheets of water that drenched all riders. But the day was turning hot. It didn't matter.

Clay and Ann Lansing rode to the chuck wagon to which Lonnie Randall had brought up a packhorse and Rose Lansing's mare, equipped with her sidesaddle. Clay and the girl pulled two heavily laden canvas bags from the wagon and lashed them on the packhorse. Rose Lansing mounted, and the three of them rode into the river, leading the pack animal. Rose Lansing, still refusing to follow her daughter's example of riding astride, adamantly ignored the inconvenience of soaked skirts as the water splashed high.

Ann Lansing had a double-barreled, sawed shotgun across the saddle and a six-shooter in a holster at her waist. Her mother also carried a pistol and had a rifle in the saddle-boot. Pedro Sanchez had a reputation for having built up his holding of cattle from the American side. His rancho was said to be a haven for outlaws.

Sanchez was waiting to meet them as they rode ashore. He lived up to his reputation, as far as appearances went, at least. He was a big, pock-marked, cold-eyed man, wearing expensive *charro* garb, with barbered sideburns and a waxed mustache.

Two more *vaqueros* had left the herd and came riding up to augment the bodyguard. They joined in the *"Buenos días!"* greeting that Sanchez uttered, taking their cue from their *patrón.*

Sanchez was mounted on a fine bay horse, astride a heavy silver-mounted saddle with a dinnerplate horn and ornate *tapaderas.* He and his men had cartridge bandoliers over their shoulders, with carbines and machetes slung on the saddles. Sanchez had a gold-hilted dagger in the red sash that circled his waist.

"Buenos días, señor," Rose Lansing said as her horse splashed to dry land. "I see you have the cattle ready."

"Si, señora," Sanchez said, beaming. "One thousand head of prime animals. I am giving them away for nothing at the price of only five dollars a head. In addition, I have thrown in a few extra. I am a generous man. They are road-branded, as you requested, and ready to be driven to market."

The man was really an American who had adopted a Mexican name and mannerisms. At least one of the three *vaqueros* was an American also.

"Did you say five dollars?" Rose Lansing said. "You are mistaken. We agreed on a price of four dollars a head."

Sanchez moaned and clapped a hand to his forehead. "Four dollars?" he cried. "You are joking, *señora.* I—"

"Four dollars," Rose Lansing said. "Take it or leave it. There are other rancheros who would be glad to do business with us at that price."

"Do you have the money, *señora?"*

"You'll get it, and in gold—after we've tallied out your cattle. We pay only for sound animals that you deliver."

Sanchez was not offended. He smiled almost admiringly. He gave an order in Spanish to one of his men who went riding away to the herd.

Clay moved in. "We'll tally before they're shoved into the river," he said to Sanchez. "Parson, you and Senor Sanchez will tally on the left. I'll count on the right, along with any man the *señor* wants to name. We pay on average count if there's any small difference. If there's a big difference we'll tally again."

That was agreeable to Sanchez. He looked at the river. Then he looked dubiously at Clay's crew. "The river is growing mean," he said. "You may have trouble. My cattle are wild."

Clay nodded. "Tell your men that I'll pay a dollar each for any that want to help shove the drive across. And tobacco."

Sanchez's bodyguards beamed and immediately volunteered. American tobacco was worth far more than the dollar as far as they were concerned. They rode away to carry the news to the *vaqueros* with the cattle.

"You're bein' a leetle free with our money, ain't you, Clay?" Beaverslide complained. "There's a whole passel of them Mex riders. Maybe a dozen or more. That'll add up to as high as fifteen dollars gone for nothin', not to mention a big hole in our tobacco stock. We kin handle this alone."

"These cattle aren't trail-broke," Clay said. "By the time we hit the rivers up north they'll be toughened to it. Better to risk a few dollars now than to regret it later. With a double crew we ought to make it without losing a head—or a man. We can stock up on tobacco later."

What he actually meant was that his crew needed to be toughened to the trail also before attempting a river crossing of this caliber. But if they knew that also, they wouldn't admit it. Ham Marsh gave a snort of scorn. Pete Fosdick squirted a stream of tobacco juice and uttered a grunt of contempt.

Bill Conners saw his chance to challenge Clay's judgment. "If you're afeared, I'll shove them cows acrost with just our own boys, Burnet," he said. "We don't need any help from them Mex."

Conners had been sullen and antagonistic, resenting being subordinated to Clay's authority. He had been palpably seeking a showdown ever since he had learned he was to be only a member of the crew instead of trail boss.

"We'll do this my way," Clay said.

Conners uttered a snort of disdain, intending to make an issue of it, but Rose Lansing spoke. "That ends the talk, Bill." Conners was forced to drop the matter.

Pedro Sanchez discovered that Ann Lansing was more than just a member of the crew. "*Hola!*" he exclaimed and swept off his bangled sombrero. "A *señorita*. This *is* a surprise."

His eyes took in her masculine attire. He moved his horse closer. Ann Lansing lifted the shotgun and pretended to take a bead on some target just beyond the man. "I'll bet a peso I can knock the top off that clump of pear," she said. "And still have a barrel left for other forms of pests."

Sanchez halted his horse. He grinned weakly. "She's what you would call a chip off the old block," he said to Rose Lansing.

It was late afternoon when the tally was completed. Rose Lansing counted out the payment in gold coins from the two canvas bags on the packhorse. Sanchez and his *vaqueros* stood by, gazing fascinated at the double eagles that she stacked in tallies of five hundred dollars each on a spread blanket.

"We'll settle for one thousand even," she said. Actually the tally had been fifteen cattle short of the agreed number, and Sanchez knew it, but he also knew that, with the river rising fast, neither Clay nor Rose Lansing would ask for a recount.

Sundown was at hand when the combined crew prepared to push the cattle into the river. The animals were wild and agile, and difficult to control. The Rio Grande had grown more ugly, more dangerous. Evidently there had been heavy storms upstream, and Clay feared that the crest of the rise had not yet arrived.

He saw some of the *vaqueros* crossing themselves as they prepared to earn the dollar and tobacco. He tried to assign his older men, such as the Parson and Beaverslide to the drag of the herd, where they would be in less danger if trouble came.

They huffily refused. "I was handlin' cows afore you was born," Beaverslide snorted. "These here air our own critters, paid fer with Rose Lansing's money, which we aim to see that she gits back. I ain't trustin' them *pelados* to try very hard at this job if'n we git into a tight squeeze."

Clay was at right point and Micah took the opposite point as the herd, strung out in a ragged column, headed down the long sloping sandbank toward the water. Clay had already picked out the leader, a rangy, rawboned, belligerent steer, the biggest in the herd. This animal had a magnificent spread of horns, and was distinguished by a band of pure white from neck to tail down its back, its hide otherwise being a rich red—a lineback, in cow parlance, but the *vaqueros* had named the animal Blanco because of the white stripe.

The cattle had been held off water all day and were thirsty and eager to cool off in the river. The Blanco steer led the way into the water, with the stronger animals at his heels. They attempted to tarry to drink, but Clay and Micah, with the help of *vaqueros*, kept them moving deeper into the current.

Blanco, a dozen yards ahead of the others, finally reached swimming depth. Clay lifted a shout. "It's going to be swimming water most of the way. Be careful. Don't let them turn back or they'll mill."

Quirts began to pop, lashing water in the faces of steers that tried to swing out of line, forcing them to stay on course. The *vaqueros*, with their long Mexican quirts, were in their element at this art. The reports of the whips were like pistol shots.

The river's direction was north to south at this point, and that put the setting sun at their backs, which was a factor in favor of success. Clay knew that cattle could be kept swimming as long as they could see their destination. The Texas shore was nearly half a mile away. The distance was broken by small islands and spits of sandbars that still stood above water, and which would offer brief respites for the cattle, but the far shore was distinct in the clear air, and the cattle could see it.

Clay's horse was swimming strongly. It was a big-bellied bay from his string of seven animals that he knew was a good water horse. He unbuckled his gunbelt and draped it around his neck, and did the same with his boots, a shift in weight that nearly capsized the horse. The animal righted itself and continued to push powerfully ahead.

Blanco reached shallow water that led to a dry sandbar and Clay's horse, along the vanguard of the herd, found bottom also, and waded ahead. Blanco willingly crossed the dry bar and moved into the river again. Clay found wading water for his horse until they were in midstream. Then the river deepened again, and the current ran stronger.

Looking back, Clay could see the herd, a long, black rope, winding across the sandbar and into the river, bending here, curving there, stretching out back of him.

A blocky, mustached, tough-jawed rider from Sanchez's crew was riding in the first swing position a dozen rods back of Clay, using his quirt and talking to the cattle, casual talk that soothed the animals. The man was speaking in Spanish, but it was broken Spanish. He was, like Sanchez, an American—an outlaw, no doubt.

Clay found the current increasing. It began to carry Blanco and the leaders downstream. He peered and saw that there was a wide expanse of water in that direction. It was an eddy where the current swung in a circle, capturing driftwood. If the cattle were carried into that swirl, they were almost certain to become confused and that would bring on that terror of river crossings—a mill.

Other riders saw the danger also. The *Americano* near Clay lifted a shout. "Keep 'em headed upstream, cowboys! They kin make it, if you squeeze 'em! Don't let 'em drift down!"

Clay, forcing his mount ahead, was already managing to turn Blanco into fighting crosswise against the current in a more direct line toward shore which was now only a hundred yards away. The *Americano* was also working furiously to achieve the same purpose with the swing of the herd.

The lineback steer seemed to sense the danger, and co-operated. The head of the long line of animals swung sluggishly back toward the shore.

Clay heard a shout of alarm. The *Americano* was in trouble. His horse apparently had caught a hoof in a stirrup and was floundering. Then the animal capsized and went under. Its rider could not swim. Clay saw the sick fear of death in the man's hard face as he tried to struggle clear. He succeeded in escaping from the struggling horse, but he then went under.

Clay left the saddle and headed for the spot where the man had vanished. Some of the steers swung out of line and began drifting downstream. Riders on the flank urged their swimming horses faster ahead to close the gap and prevent others from following.

Clay was caught among the animals that had left the column. The cattle were splashing water and snorting and bawling in a panic. He fought his way among them to where he judged the man had gone down. He was forced to dive among thrashing hoofs. A hoof grazed an arm, another struck his leg where the arrow wound was still tender.

Forcing his eyes to stay open, he sighted a shape in the

murky water. It was the *Americano*. He grabbed the man
and fought his way to the surface. He was starved for air,
and weakening, but he managed to lift the head of the
man clear of the water. The *Americano* wheezed and
coughed, but he was alive, and oxygen revived him enough
to respond to Clay's gasped order not to struggle.

The current carried them, along with the loose cattle,
into the big eddy. Clay treaded water desperately in order
to support his burden. He was at the end of his strength
when the eddy carried them near shore. Micah was there.
He had left his horse and stood waist-deep whirling his
lariat. His cast settled expertly around Clay.

Clay found himself being pulled ashore along with his
burden. Reaching shallow water he looked up at Micah,
trying to grin. "Good throw," he gasped. "I was running
out of ambition."

He struggled to his knees and peered. The bulk of the
herd was under control and beginning to stream ashore
well above the eddy. The animals that had drifted into the
pool were still struggling. *Vaqueros* and Patchsaddle men
came riding to help, and began roping animals that came
within reach. But many were going down, giving up the
struggle.

Ann Lansing was among the arrivals. She swung down
from her horse, looking at Clay, then at the man he had
saved from the river. "What were you trying to prove?"
she demanded, her voice shrill. "You should be dead. You
know that. Look at you! You're bleeding!"

The blows from hoofs that had seemed so inconsequential
under water had ripped a gash in Clay's left shoulder. The
arrow wound had been reopened.

Rose Lansing rode up and dismounted. "Another bandaging job," she said tersely. "Help me, Ann."

She too gazed accusingly at Clay. "You shouldn't have
tried it, you know," she said. "It was a big risk. Why?"

Clay was asking himself whether Ann Lansing might not

have answered that question already. Had he really been trying to prove something, prove that he had a right to the tranquillity that he had been seeking so vainly since that day at Hatcher's Run—that morning when the cannon roar was an affliction no human nerves or human ears should be forced to hear—that morning when he had ordered Phil Lansing to his death?

Vaqueros and Americans were reviving the man he had saved in the river. Rough jests were uttered as they pumped water from his lungs. They thumped and belabored him until he was breathing normally.

Finally the man sat up, propping himself weakly on his arms, watching Rose and Ann Lansing bandage Clay's injuries. "*Gracias*," he said to Clay.

"*Da nada*," Clay said, grinning, using the polite Spanish phrase. "It was nothing."

"It was a lot to me," the man said, abandoning any pretense that he was Mexican. "I'd be food for the gars by this time. I'll make it up to you some day."

"There's nothing to be made up," Clay said. "Forget it."

"Could you use another hand on the drive?" the man asked. "I'd work for nothing."

"We could use a good hand," Clay said. "And you'll be paid, if you really want to go up the trail. What's your name?"

The man showed a trace of a sardonic grin. He thought it over for moment. "*Sabe*," he said. "That's the last name."

"First name's *Quién*, I take it," Clay said. "Who knows."

"It's as good as any," the man said.

"If you ride with us, you take care of your own miseries," Clay said. "We've got worries enough without loading mistakes in the past onto the chuck wagon. Is that clear?"

"I *sabe*," the man said.

"If so, I'll cut you a saddle string when we get squared away," Clay said. "We pay off at the end of the drive. We expect every rider to hold up his end of the work."

The man moved away to care for his saddle, which the *vaqueros* had retrieved from the drowned horse in the river. Ann Lansing spoke indignantly. "What do you mean by giving that man a job? He's an outlaw. It's written all over him. And that name *Quién Sabe*. He's probably wanted by every sheriff on this side of the river."

"He's tough," Clay said. "Made of leather and catgut by the looks. We'll be needing more of that kind before we're through with this affair."

"I won't stand for—"

Her mother spoke gently. "Mr. Burnet is foreman. He will do the hiring as he sees fit."

"And the firing," Clay said.

And so *Quién Sabe*, or Q, as the others began calling him, joined the Patchsaddle crew. Clay judged that he was about forty, and the history of a violent life was written on his scarred face and a nose that had been broken many times. But, outlaw or not, in him was that vital thing which for a better name was called character.

Rose Lansing paid off the *vaqueros* in silver dollars from the common fund and gave pouches of tobacco to each man from the stores in the supply wagon. "The cost will be apportioned among us at trail's end," she told the San Dimas men as they watched the whooping *vaqueros* head back across the river.

CHAPTER 5

Clay rode in the supply wagon with Rachel and Cindy for a few days until he was able to take saddle again. The Mexican cattle were trailed slowly, carefully northward to the Lansing ranch, where the cattle of the various brands from the San Dimas pool were being held by men who were not making the drive north.

The united herd was given three days to settle down, and two more days of casual driving to permit the animals to become accustomed to the presence of riders and to discipline. The morning came when Clay awakened before daybreak and began beating on the dishpan that Rose Lansing had hung on a nail on the chuck wagon.

"Rise and shine!" he yelled. "School's over. So's the fun. Today we head 'em north for keeps. Roll your spurs, men. Today you become trail drivers."

Beaverslide Smith rolled out of his bed and came groaning to his feet on aching, complaining bones. He uttered a quavering Confederate yell to prove that his spirit was willing, even if the flesh was weak. The others exhibited equal enthusiasm, some real, some feigned. Clay could see that doubts were already beginning to arise among some of the Patchsaddle crew.

He discovered that one man was still in his blankets. He had stirred, then had turned over, resolutely burying his head in the blanket. He was Bill Conners, the malcontent.

In his career as a prizefighter in the past, Conners had survived savage, bare-knuckle endurance contests that lasted until one or the other opponent admitted defeat or could no longer stand on his feet. He bore the scars of those days, bore them boastfully. He had held down riding jobs at the Lansing ranch between bouts, and had gravitated into the foreman's job at the end of the war mainly by default, since there were few men around to choose from.

It was evident he longed to prove his boxing ability, with Clay as his target. Clay had assigned him to the last night shift, which was regarded as one of the most responsible, for herds on bedground were more prone to restlessness and to stampeding in the predawn hours when the animal world was on the prowl, particularly natural enemies such as wolves and cougars.

Conners had not finished out his shift, and had come in alone to turn in, leaving the responsibility to the other two riders. These were Pete Fosdick and Jess Randall. Their blankets were still vacant, showing that they had remained with the herd, a task that would continue until the entire crew rode out to throw the cattle on the trail.

Desertion of a herd green to the trail was akin to a mortal sin in the code of cattlemen. In this case it was a calculated challenge to Clay's authority. Around them the other men were pretending not to be aware of what was happening. They were making a great show of yanking on their boots, of going to the nearby creek, and of dousing water on their faces.

But they knew! Ann Lansing knew also. She had appeared from the small tent attached to the supply wagon, which served as sleeping quarters for herself and her mother. Her face held the residue of restful slumber and forgotten dreams. She was plaiting her hair into the customary two pigtails, which she would form into buns that would fit beneath the sombrero she wore on the trail.

She gazed at Clay, and there was something like pity in her eyes. She had known that this was inevitable, and that now the moment had come. Clay had known it also. By reason of his rank, he slept beneath the chuck wagon where he was sheltered from weather, while the men of crew took their chances under tarps if rain came. It was the foreman's privilege. He had left his belt and holstered six-shooter hanging on a wagon strut until time to mount. He walked to it now, lifted the belt, strapped it on and nudged the holster into a comfortable position.

He heard men draw sighing breaths and look for cover as they began edging away. They all knew Conners had a pistol concealed under his blankets, and that he had only been feigning sleep, and was ready for this showdown.

It was Ann Lansing who came out of the trance that held the camp. She rushed at Clay and tried to snatch the Colt from his holster. He backed away, defeating that purpose.

"No!" she cried shrilly. "There's no need for anyone being killed! Haven't you seen enough of that?"

There it was again—the question. The question her mother had wanted to ask so many times. How had Phil Lansing died?

Clay turned and walked to where Conners still lay in his blankets. "Get up, Conners," he said. "Quit playing possum. I know you're awake."

Conners came out of his blankets. He was fully dressed, even to his boots. He got to his feet, but the six-shooter he had taken to bed with him still lay there, and he moved out of reach of it. "What do you want, Burnet?" he asked. It was evident that, of all things, he did not want a gunfight now that Clay was armed and ready.

"Rig your horse and pull out," Clay said. "Don't linger for breakfast. We don't feed bunch quitters."

"You can't fire me," Conners said. Fury was a storm in him. The ache to mash Clay with his fists was shaking him, crimsoning his heavy jowls, knotting his fists.

"It's got to be that way," Clay said. "You pushed this. You know I can't let you get away with this."

"Take that gun off you," Conners said. "Then we'll see how big you talk. I'll show you who's the best man in this drive. I'm the one that's entitled to ride as foreman, an' you to stand night guard."

Clay unbuckled his gunbelt and hung the weapon on the chuck wagon. He returned to face Conners.

"No, Bill!" Rose Lansing cried. "Stop it! He's no match for you, and you know it. He's injured, and he's still limping."

Conners paid no heed. The hunger to right the wrongs he believed had been done was too keen. He came moving in on Clay with the poise of a skilled boxer. He was big, with the litheness of a horseman.

Even so, Clay was able to weather the first storm and do some damage. He blocked the first heavy punches that Conners threw, and drove a right to the throat that drove the man back, fish-mouthed. But Conners came in again, punching. Clay found his injured leg giving way under him. He could hear Rose Lansing screaming for Conners to stop.

His leg buckled, and Conners caught him with solid punches. He felt nausea. He managed to duck a knockout blow that came at his jaw and staggered forward, driving his head into Conners' stomach. Both went down. The breath gushed from the bigger man, and his flailing arms lost power.

Clay realized that Rose Lansing was trying to pull them apart. "Help me, you idiots!" she gasped. "They'll kill each other."

Men moved in and ended the fight. Clay sat up, too spent to move. Conners finally got to his feet.

"Rig your horse, Bill," Rose Lansing said. "Get out of camp as fast as you can."

"That's a harsh way to treat a man who's been foreman of your ranch," Conners said.

He bundled his bedroll, shoved his effects into the canvas bag that served as his war sack, and saddled and mounted his personal horse.

"You'll regret this," he said to Rose Lansing. "An' so will you, Burnet." Then he rode out of camp.

The man they called Q moved to Clay's side. "I better trail him aways to make sure he keeps headin' south," he murmured.

"No need," Clay said. "It's over."

"That I doubt," Q said. "That feller has a black grudge workin' inside him. Things like that fester 'til they become pure poison. I know the kind. He could turn into a killer."

Clay shrugged it away. He signaled for Lonnie Randall to bring up the *remuda*. The crew moved out, ropes dangling, to cut their first mounts from their strings for the start of the day's drive.

"Your hawss, boss," Lonnie said importantly, roping and leading up Clay's first mount. "You sure took care o' that big shorthorn. Good riddance. You should have put a bullet in him."

"How old are you, Lonnie?" Clay asked. "It's a question I've been wanting to put since we left the San Dimas, but I've been too busy to get around to it."

"I'm goin' on eighteen," Lonnie said. He drew from a shirt pocket a tobacco sack and started to roll a brown paper smoke. The result was not what he had planned. It more resembled a crumpled leaf.

Ann Lansing walked in, plucked the quirlie from his hand, and confiscated the sack of tobacco. "He's not quite sixteen," she told Clay, "and ought to be in school."

"Aw shucks, Ann," Lonnie moaned. "I saw all the school I want. *Years* of it. You was my teacher when I was a yearlin'. Now I'm the best damned horse jingler—"

"From now on," Ann said, "I'll be your teacher again. You'll do a little studying while you're loafing along with the *remuda*. It happens that I brought some books along just for you and Cindy."

"I'd just like to see you try to—" Lonnie began.

Clay reached out, caught him by the belt, and hop-scotched him stiff-legged to stand directly in front of Ann Lansing. "Say 'yes ma'am,'" he said. "Say you'll be mighty glad to have her waste her time trying to drive some book learning into that knothead of yours. Say it."

Lonnie was lifted almost bodily from the ground so that he was ignominiously spider-legged. "Yes ma'am!" he managed to gurgle. "If the big augur says so, I'll do my best, no matter how it hurts."

Clay released him. Lonnie's father was standing by, grinning. "I couldn't prevail on him to stay home," Jess Randall explained. "He said he'd follow us up the trail, an' he'd have done it too. He's knotheaded, like you said. Takes after his mother for strong will. So I figgered it better to let him ride along. He'll earn his keep."

"See that you earn your own," Clay said. "You were on late nighthawk along with Pete Fosdick and Bill Conners this morning. You let a string of loafers drift loose. What were you doing, sleeping in the saddle, like Conners was in his bed?"

"Cattle? No loafers got by me!" Randall declared.

Clay pointed. In the brightening light of day a scattered band of some score of cattle were visible, meandering south over the back trail of the drive. They were a mile or more away, but in no hurry.

"Fetch 'em in," Clay said. "You and Fosdick. You lost 'em, you bring 'em in. Any that are missing when we tally next time will be charged up to you two when we settle up at the finish."

He walked away amid silence. When he spoke again, ordering them to saddle and throw the herd on the trail they moved with alacrity. Fosdick and Jess Randall brought in the loose cattle by riding extra miles and enduring the badgering of comrades who were, in fact, secretly thanking their lucky stars that they had not been caught in the same situation.

"You're being a little hard on them, aren't you?" Rose Lansing asked Clay.

"That's nothing to how I'll rawhide them if it happens again," Clay answered.

Ann Lansing spoke. "Maybe you're only trying to act important. Maybe being named trail boss has gone to your head. It happens that Bill Conners doesn't own any of these cattle, but the most of the others have a stake in this drive. It's their stock to lose if they make a mistake."

"And their lives," Clay said. "I don't want any more of that on—"

He broke off, mounted and rode away. Once more he had almost said too much. Once more it was all back before him—that grisly day on the battlefield.

He rode hipshot on the ambling horse. The fight with Bill Conners was two weeks in the past and fading from memory. He looked only at the peace of the moment, knowing that it would not last. The cattle were tractable, the weather mild. Grass was rich and greening. He had talked to men who had traveled north. He had hand-drawn maps in his pockets and had memorized verbal descriptions of what lay ahead. There would be sufficient water for the next two or three days. Then would come the first real test.

They were crossing the mighty Edwards Plateau, and a sixty-mile dry stretch lay ahead, with the gamble that the creek they hoped to reach might be dry also. It was a risk drovers from South Texas always faced. The majority won. Some lost.

Slowly the interlude of peace of mind drained away. He rode listlessly, completely alone even amid the droning, ceaseless presence of life around him, of the rattle of hundreds of hoofs in motion, of the intermittent call of a swing man turning a stubborn animal back into line, of the ever-present bawling of bovine protest. It was a massive host that moved with him, and its fate was all in his hands. All the decisions would be his, as it had been that day at Hatcher's Run.

The chuck wagon rolled along abreast of the leaders of the drive, with Rose Lansing handling the reins of the mules. Rachel followed on the supply wagon with Cindy beside her on the seat.

Cindy held aloft a papermade whirligig that her mother had formed and had pinned to a long, slender branch. The toy began revolving dizzily in the warm morning breeze. Clay could see the bright delight in Cindy's face as she watched the success of the improvised plaything. He was long to remember that joy, that young, innocent moment of happiness.

Then the herd stampeded. One moment the cattle had been complacently peaceful. The next instant they had become a frightful juggernaut, mindless, deadly. They had run a few times in the past several days, but these had only been halfhearted efforts that had died of lack of interest. This was the real thing.

Clay touched his horse with steel, hoping to turn Blanco and the leaders. He carried with him as he rode little Cindy's sudden change of expression. Her joy had shifted to fright and self-accusation. She believed the whirligig had spooked the herd.

One of the San Dimas men, Tom Gary, was riding into the teeth of the avalanche, firing his six-shooter across the faces of the leaders in an attempt to turn them. Then his horse pitched head over heels.

Clay saw Gary's body being flung free. Then he vanished beneath a flood of horns, hoofs, and dust.

The panic faded after the cattle had run for nearly five miles. The scattered animals, as though obeying a single impulse, slowed to a trot, then to a walk. They halted and began grazing.

Clay rode back to the place where Tom Gary had gone down. Other Patchsaddle men were already there. Ann

Lansing was approaching, her face ashen. Clay waved her back.

"Go to Rachel and 'specially to Cindy," he said. "They will need someone with them. Tell Cindy the run was started by a coyote, or a rattlesnake. Make her believe it. *Make her believe it!* She might have to live with this the rest of her life. With ghosts."

They buried Tom Gary on higher ground in a coffin of green planks that the crew sawed from cottonwoods. Parson Jones intoned the invocation. Rose and Ann Lansing sang a hymn. Rachel, holding Cindy's hand, joined in.

". . . yet shall he live," the Parson said. "Amen!"

They repeated a final prayer together. Clay and four other men fired a soldier's volley over the grave, for Tom Gary had worn the gray. Gary had been a quiet, reserved man with whom Clay had little more than a casual acquaintance. He was leaving a widow and two children back in the San Dimas, and it came to Clay that the location of this grave in this lonely land would be forgotten soon.

He turned away from the grave. He had turned away from so many graves, heard the crash of so many volleys for the departed soldiers. It was over. Over for all, he thought, except small Cindy. The child had stood forlorn during the services. In spite of all attempts to solace her, she believed the toy she had so innocently held to the warm breeze in her moment of happiness had caused Tom Gary's death.

Clay took the child's hand, walked to where he had left his horse and lifted her astride across the animal's neck. He mounted and rode to where there were no cattle, no humans. Only the peace of the great plain.

He felt the taut agony in the child as she leaned against him. He felt the deep quiver of grief, of despair in her. "Once upon a time," he said. "I was a soldier. I was in a battle. It was a place called Hatcher's Run. Back in that country a creek was called a 'run.' It was a long, long way from here. It would take a month to ride to Hatcher's Run.

We were losing the battle. The other side had more guns, more men. They were men just like me."

"Why was you fightin' them?" Cindy asked.

Clay was at a loss for an answer. It was a question he had asked himself many times. He had asked it during the fury of a dozen battles. He had asked it at Hatcher's Run, but he had never found an answer that was really an answer.

"I guess you'd call it pride," he finally said. "I guess neither side wanted to admit they were wrong, or that the other might be the best fighter. Something happened that day that still makes me very sad when I remember it. Sometimes it even makes me want to cry."

"Cry?" Cindy echoed incredulously. "But you are a man— a big man. You are the trail boss. Big men don't cry."

"Sometimes a man wishes he could," Clay said. "I was an officer, a captain. That's a sort of a trail boss. My outfit was surrounded by Yanks. We were protecting a battery of cannon that were very valuable to our side. There was only one way to save the guns. We had to create a diversion. That means making the other side think you're going one way when you really are taking off in the other direction. That also meant sending some of our own men to do this. There wasn't much chance any of them would come back alive. I couldn't go myself. I had two hundred men in my crew and it was up to me to see that as many of them as possible got out of that fix they were in, along with the cannon. I had to pick the men who would likely be killed. It happened that the man who was the only one who could lead a thing like that was not my friend. His family and mine had not been friends for years."

"Like the Lansings an' the Burnets?" Cindy asked.

Clay tried to look at her, but decided that her small, young face was innocent of any accusing knowledge.

"Yes," he said, his voice becoming hoarse and shaky, now that the memories were back in full flood. "This soldier was young and very popular with the men in the ranks, maybe much better liked than I was. That's one of the penalties for being the trail boss. I had to order him to lead the diversion. He knew it was an order for him to die. Everybody knew it. I saw it in his eyes, and in theirs, that they believed I was doing it because we were not friends. He never came back from where I sent him, nor did the eleven other men I ordered to their deaths. But they succeeded in saving me and the other two hundred, and the cannon. They drew the enemy away from one point long enough for us to fight our way out of the trap and get back to our main lines."

Cindy looked up at him, and tears were glistening on her small face. She was sobbing. She said nothing, but he knew that, young as she was, she understood his torture just as he understood her own travail. And she knew why he had talked to her, talked as though she was a grown-up who needed consolation, just as he needed consolation.

"I'm sure they're in heaven," she wept. "Jest like I pray that Mister Gary is in heaven."

"Never blame yourself, Cindy," Clay said. "Many things might have brought on the stampede. Many things that we don't know about."

Ann Lansing rode up and lifted Cindy onto her own horse. She studied Clay briefly, then moved away, asking no questions. Clay followed her. In the distance men were filling the grave and rolling up boulders to protect it. Rose Lansing and Rachel returned to the wagons, and with the help of men who swamped for them, were preparing to hook up the teams and move to the next night's camp.

The roundup of scattered cattle began. The bulk of the herd had clung together, but several hundred animals had seized the chance to again head south for home. They were overtaken and brought back by weary men on tired horses. By sundown the herd was mainly intact again. Half a dozen animals had been killed, their carcasses already torn

by coyotes and buzzards. Clay judged that perhaps a dozen
more were missing and would become prey to the wolves,
or would join the mavericks that wandered in the wild
draws and thickets.

He rode slowly around the bedground. The cattle were at
peace once more. Downwind, the breeze brought the stale,
wild smell of the Longhorns, their body heat, the knowledge
that here was a mindless force as elemental and impersonal
as the wind, the stars, the sun, a force that had already
taken one life and could take more.

Clay picked out a prime young steer and cut it from the
herd. "Beef it," he told Dad Hoskins, who acted as cook's
helper, swamper, and butcher, as well as assistant horse
wrangler. "Let it cure until ready. Until further orders
everybody eats good steaks. All they want. And at breakfast
too."

Ann Lansing looked questioningly at him. The custom
was that inferior stock, the lame and crippled, serve as fare
on the drive. Strong cattle with tallow on their bones graded
up a herd, and the more of them the better the price would
be for the entire herd of the bidding grounds were ever
reached.

"Men last longer on dry drives if they're on good fodder
at the start," he said. "So do cattle."

The dry drive was ahead. Clay had sent Micah north
three days earlier to scout the way, and the big black man
had returned, saddle-worn, thirsty with dry canteens, and
on a spent horse, in time to attend Tom Gary's burial.

"Tuk me more'n a day to reach watah enough to fill a
herd," he had told Clay. "Only a seep in between. Rain
water caught in rock tanks, but dryin' up, an' hardly more'n
enough at that to take care o' the saddle stock."

"How much time for a cow to walk to this running water?" Clay had asked.

"Three days, maybe," Micah said. "Less if'n you keep 'em
walkin' nights."

CHAPTER 6

They let the cattle graze for two days on the feed that grew around the marshy stream on which they were camped. They filled all canteens, pans, and kettles in the wagons. Clay awakened the men two hours before daybreak, and they threw the herd on the trail under the light of a waning moon.

The quirts began cracking. "Hi-yuh! Hi-yuh! No yuh don't, yuh jug-headed critter. Back in line. Hi-yuh! Git movin'. Hi-yuh!"

The drive strung out once again. Blanco marched in the lead. The strong young steers made a pretense at breaking line, but it was only a show, and they stepped out in the big steer's wake. The other cattle followed, the meek, the humble.

The wagons surged ahead, made a breakfast camp where riders ate hurriedly and swigged coffee in relays. Clay was the last to partake. Ann Lansing was cooling coffee also, taking respite from her place with the drive.

"Are you all right, Cindy?" she asked the child.

Cindy was grave-eyed, older in aspect. She remembered Tom Gary. "Yes, Miss Ann," she replied.

"There's a settlement called Fort Worth that will be within reach in a few days," Ann said. "I'm riding in when we get there to buy supplies and maybe a new dress for you. Would you like to go with me? It won't be far out of our way."

"I'd like that, Miss Ann."

Clay was aware that Ann Lansing was studying both

himself and the child. Again he was sure she wanted to ask a question. Then she decided not to try to pry into whatever secrets he and Cindy had exchanged.

He returned to the herd. He pushed the pace. By mid-afternoon he estimated that the cattle had walked twenty miles. He kept them moving. Twilight came, and darkness settled. He was gambling now against the chance of a stampede. In the bovine scheme of things, darkness multiplied the long rosary of imaginary terrors that even daylight held.

The animals began to bawl and grow sullen. Flank men were riding continuously to maintain discipline and hold the line. Drag men were wearing out horses each hour. Lonnie Randall and Dad Hoskins grew bone-weary as they kept meeting the demand to replace jaded horses with fresher mounts from the *remuda*.

The moon came up, and Clay finally gave the order to throw the herd off. The cattle grazed on scant forage and milled restlessly in futile search of water. The night air had turned cool, but dry. There was none of the dew Clay had hoped for on the grass that might have eased the situation.

He let them bed for five hours. Every man in the crew slept with his boots on, night horses tethered within reach. Clay slept not at all, maintaining a constant circle around the bedground to reinforce the shifts of men who stood watch.

He looked at his watch. The half moon was bright in the sky at three o'clock, the air keen and bracing. The slow draw of breeze brought the fresh tangy spice of sage and grass as he reluctantly gave the word.

"Hi-yuh!"

Sleep-drugged men, mumbling thickly and hopelessly staggered out of their blankets, clawed bedrolls into a sem-blance of order, carried them to the wagon where Rachel and Dad Hoskins were backing the mules to the swingles. Ham Marsh, whose girth was now beginning to dwindle, moved like a man in a daze, but he was moving. Clay particularly watched Uncle Cal Pryer. He was a patriarchal, gentle-speaking man who had never mentioned his age, but Clay was sure he was older than Beaverslide and the Parson. He was thin and long-geared, and his straggly gray beard fluttered in the wind. Clay could hear Uncle Cal's teeth chattering, could see him shaking with the cold. He watched the old man try twice before he could pull himself into the saddle after he had quaffed coffee and refused any other choice of breakfast. He wanted Uncle Cal to give up, turn back for home. He had suggested that as diplomatically as he could a day or so previously.

Uncle Cal had stiffened with hurt pride. "Maybe I ain't quite as spry as you, Burnet," he had said, "but I can still fork a bronc and spill a loop along with any of you younger whippersnappers. An' I'll drink all of you under the table when we hit this here Missouri."

Ann Lansing came from the wagon, carrying an extra cup of coffee for Uncle Cal. He refused to accept it. "Don't need it, Annie girl," he said, bracing himself crisply erect in the saddle. "Give it to old Pete Fosdick over there. He looks like he's goin' to shiver hisself right out'n his skin."

She gave Clay a hopeless look and turned away. Micah, who was riding swing as the herd was thrown on the trail in the pale morning light, began to sing softly in his deep voice:

As I was walkin' down de street,
    Down de street, down de street,
A handsome gal I chanced to meet, chanced to meet,
    Oh, she was fair to view.

Ann Lansing's clear contralto joined in from somewhere down the line, and the voices of more riders took up the refrain.

Buffalo gals, can't you come out tonight,
    Can't you come out tonight,
    And dance by the light of the moon?

The nervous bawling of the cattle faded. The singing soothed them, and they struck out in the wake of Blanco and the lead steers.

Dawn came, pink, then bright golden. Clay had been hoping, praying, for clouds, for rain. His supplication was not fulfilled. The chill of dawn faded. The day was turning hot. He sent word down the line to let the cattle graze as they moved, but to never let them stop.

"How far?" he asked Micah at noon.

They were moving across a rolling plain that had no horizons, no offer of mercy to men or cattle. It was a brassy gridiron on which they seemed to make no progress. Weaker cattle were lagging, and Clay assigned more riders to the drag. Wolves and buzzards were following the herd.

Canteens were about exhausted. At midafternoon Rose Lansing and Rachel managed a tepid drink, flavored with brown sugar and lemon extract with the last water in the cooking supply. It was at least liquid and offered some nourishment. There was nothing for the cattle and horses. The tanks of rain water that Micah had found on his scouting trip had vanished.

They pushed on past the drying mud of the tanks with the sun beating down savagely as the afternoon advanced. Clay touched his listless horse with his knees suddenly, lifting it into a shuffling trot. He reached the side of Uncle Cal Pryer in time to catch him before he toppled from the saddle.

Micah came riding to help. Between them they carried Uncle Cal to the wagon where Rachel and Rose Lansing were waiting with cloths they had dampened in water that Rachel had held out for just such an emergency.

It was too late. Uncle Cal looked up at Clay and tried to grin. "No regrets," he said. "Don't blame yourself, you young whippersnapper. This is the way fer a cowboy to go, ridin' with his pals, with spurs on his boots, an' the cattle headin' north. Buy thet drink for the boys for me when you hit Missoury, Clay."

Then he was gone. Rachel and Rose Lansing covered their faces and sobbed. After a time Clay stood up. The cattle were still moving stolidly ahead. Their dismal lowing was a dirge. The outriders were peering toward the wagon, not knowing exactly what had happened, fearing to learn.

Clay waved them ahead. The drive must go on. "Uncle Cal would be the first to say that," he said hoarsely to anyone who would listen. "He'd say to keep 'em moving."

Dad Hoskins had left the *remuda* to come in to the wagons. He had seen Uncle Cal die. He and Cal Pryer had been lifelong friends. As young men they had fought under Sam Houston in the Texas war for independence from Mexico. They had been at San Jacinto the day Santa Anna's army had been wiped out.

Dad Hoskins glared at Rose Lansing. His beard was as gray and wind-blown as had been that of Uncle Cal. His hands were gnarled by saddle work and rheumatism. Time was bending his shoulders.

"I blame you, Rosemary," he said hoarsely, and tears were on his seamed cheeks. "First Tom Gary, an' now Cal Pryer. You was the one that kept naggin' an' tauntin' us. Cal told you that he was too old, when you prodded him. You laughed an' told him it'd be better to die livin' like a man than to keep on rottin' in poverty in a shack. Look at him! Look at what you done! You'll have this on your soul, Rosemary, as long—"

"No," Clay broke in. "Mrs. Lansing was right. Uncle Cal died happy—a proud man. He was here, among his own kind. He had been *alive* these days on the trail. He wanted to do this. He'd have died in shame if he stayed behind. He was a cattleman. He died among his own kind. Don't blame her. Don't blame anyone. She gave him the right to die proud of himself. You don't know what you're doing, trying to brand her guilty of killing a human being. *You don't know!"*

He walked to his horse and mounted. "Put Uncle Cal in the bedwagon," he said huskily. "We'll bury him when we camp."

He rode back to the herd. He carried with him the memory of Rose Lansing standing over Uncle Cal Pryer's body, her hands clasped, complete agony and grief in her face. His words had failed to console her. She blamed herself.

He rode like a demon the rest of the day, changing horses often, keeping Lonnie Randall busy furnishing him with fresh mounts. He drove the cattle. He drove men. He spent the greater part of the time with the drag where the weaker animals were falling farther and farther behind. Normally there would be only a score or so of cattle in the drag, needing only the presence of one rider to haze them along. Now there were more than a hundred animals straggling along in the wake of the main herd, with three riders working to keep them moving.

The westering sun had no mercy. Clay shot a cow that had gone down and could not rise. Better that than to leave the animal to be torn apart alive by the gray shadows that were following the herd in force now, and by the black wedges floating in the sky.

It was a duty he repeated again and again before sundown. "Keep 'em moving," he told the men from a throat cracked and parched. "How far, Micah?"

"Five miles," the black man said. "Maybe farther. I cain't exactly locate myself. Every danged gully an' clump o' brush looks like what I seen an hour ago."

They drove on in twilight, in darkness, for hours. The glow of the old, fading moon was beginning to show in the east when the cattle caught the scent of water. The terrible moaning that had been a hymn of agony changed to a wild roar.

There was no holding them. "Ride clear!" Clay shouted. "Let 'em run!"

At least it was only cattle that died in the terrible race for water, and not men. A few more animals drowned in the crush as the herd piled into the bed of the creek, churning it into a froth of mud.

Clay rode upstream on his jaded horse until he found a pool of unsullied water. It glinted like a great diamond in the first strike of moonlight. He fell limply from his horse, crawled to the brink, and slumped forward on his face in the resurrecting coolness of the stream.

After a time he realized that someone had followed his example. Ann Lansing lay nearby, drinking prayerfully. She loosened her hair and let it float free in the water. Using her hands for cups, she drenched herself and kept making that grateful little sound of thanks.

Satiated at last, she flirted water from her hair and let it hang down her back while she sat up and looked at him. "I'm sorry," she said.

"Sorry? For what?"

"For, for many things. That yellow ribbon, for one."

"I've still got it," Clay said. "Waiting for a candidate. But there's been none."

"I'm afraid there soon will be," she said. "Some of the men are talking of quitting."

"Let them," Clay said.

"Mother is desolate," she said. "She blames herself for Uncle Cal, and for Tom Gary. She wants to turn back, if we can."

"There's no turning back now."

She was silent for a moment. "I want to thank you," she finally said. "For telling them it wasn't her fault. Otherwise I don't know what she'd have done. She's taking Uncle Cal's death very hard."

"He died happy," Clay said. "She must understand that."

She was silent a moment. "You were in command of the

company in which Phil was a sergeant during the last campaign of the war, weren't you?" she asked abruptly.

Clay had to force himself to answer. "Yes."

"Were you in the last battle?" she asked slowly.

"I was there."

She hesitated a long time before speaking again. "Do you want to tell me about it?" she finally asked.

Clay had faced this moment many times in his thoughts, searching for an answer and finding none. It had haunted him all those months before he found that he had fallen helplessly in love with Ann Lansing. Now the spike in his heart was driven deeper.

"No," he said harshly. "What good would it do? Men are forced into situations in war that can't ever be understood by others, and never can be forgiven."

He walked to his horse which had drunk its fill, mounted, and rode back to the herd alone, leaving Ann Lansing there —and also alone.

They dug their second grave the next morning and laid Uncle Cal to rest. On that same day they lost more men from the crew. Pete Fosdick and Dave Wilson decided that the trail was no place for them. After standing beside the grave, they came to Clay and said they'd had enough and were heading back to the San Dimas.

"An' the rest o' you better do the same," Pete Fosdick told the remainder of the crew, who were listening. "We've already buried pore Tom Gary an' Uncle Cal an' this drive ain't even half way. There'll be more graves to fill if'n you keep goin'. Rosemary Lansing sweet-talked us into this. Bein' a woman, she don't have to ride stampedes or stay in the saddle eighteen hours a day. She don't have to be rawhided by a foreman who's managed to git two of us dead already."

Ann Lansing walked up to Fosdick, who was a thin-necked, hook-nosed man. "That's not true, and you know it, Pete," she said. She turned to the others. "If any or all of you are thinking the same, either about my mother or about Clay Burnet, now's the time to say so and cut your string to head for home."

There was silence for a space. Then two more men moved to join Fosdick and Dave Wilson. One was Ike Turner, the other Dad Hoskins.

Parson Ezra Jones spoke harshly. "Go on home, you yaller-bellied leppies! None o' you was worth a pint o' sour beans anyway. Tell yore kids an' womenfolk to pin the ribbons on you. You know the color."

"What about our cattle?" Fosdick demanded. "I got forty head in the bunch. Dad's got none, but Ike an' Dave's got enough. More'n a hundred, all told."

"Take 'em back with you," Clay said.

"You know we cain't do that," Fosdick said. "No cow could walk back acrost thet dry stretch after what you put us through."

Rose Lansing spoke. "You'll be paid for them at whatever price we get when the herd is sold. After all expenses are paid we will share in proportion to the number of cattle each of us has in the herd. We signed a paper, remember, on which all brands owned by you and the rest of us are designated."

"I don't reckon we'll ever see a cent for our cattle, but we ought to git somethin' considerin' that we've already risked our necks bringin' 'em this far," Fosdick said. "We figure we ought to be paid off right now. We know you got some money in the fund, Rosemary."

"Get out of camp as fast as you can and be damned to you!" Ann Lansing exploded. "Before I take a quirt to you."

"Daughter!" her mother spoke reprovingly. "Don't forget you're a lady."

Ann Lansing looked down at herself, at her dusty chaps, her hands, her general appearance. She looked at her mother and at Rachel. Rachel had given up after the first week, and had stored away her petticoats and skirts and had retailored masculine jeans to fit her good figure. She had managed to give the jeans a jaunty Mexican style, with a slashed bell bottom effect, and had added to the picture with a colorful calico waist and gingham sash. But Rose Lansing had held out. She still wore ground-length, voluminous skirts, and her waist was obviously reinforced by stays and whalebone. Both she and Rachel had on the floursack aprons that were the badges of their servitude when meals were being prepared.

Ann's eyes traveled over the crew, taking in their patched garb, their dog-eared, rundown boots, their general appearance of having been thrown together in a ragbag. She looked at Clay. He had fared little better. His injuries had all healed but he had paid a greater penalty, at least to his garb, than the others during the hard journey.

She began to laugh. "I beg your pardon, gentlemen," she said. "I'll try to be a lady from now on, no matter what I look like."

She laughed harder, wildly at first, then with full-throated, vast, and healthy amusement. Rachel joined in. Micah's deep bass chuckle started and increased to rolling thunder. Clay began to laugh.

Beaverslide uttered a yelp. He and the Parson clasped hands and began a wild, heel-kicking buck and wing.

"Missouri, here we come!" Beaverslide howled. "We're the Patchsaddle boys, an' we ain't quittin' until we git there."

Other men joined in. The camp became a madhouse of cavorting humans, some of whom might have passed as scarecrows.

Rotund Ham Marsh took Rose Lansing's hands and started to whirl her. Startled, stiff, for an instant, she suddenly began to laugh and let herself be swung wildly, the hem of her skirt flying. This, she realized, was more than a dance. It was a memorial to their comrades who had died.

Clay found Ann Lansing standing before him, her green eyes alight. "Missouri, here we come!" she cried.

He caught her hands and they joined the rigadoon. Lonnie Randall struck up a tune with his harmonica and Jess Randall joined in with a fiddle. On the bedground, the cattle, which needed no guarding after the rigors of the dry drive, gazed with bovine surprise, horns glinting in the sun.

The four men who were leaving all this withdrew to a safer distance. "They're loco," Pete Fosdick assured his companions. "They've gone clean off their rockers. We're lucky to be shed of 'em."

CHAPTER 7

"I might be able to round up a few hands," Q said to Clay the next day.

Clay eyed him. "Where?"

"I'd need a little time," Q said. "I might be gone as long as a week. I might find 'em, I might not. But it's worth a try. You can't drive ahead with six men, an' most of 'em old an' creaky. You've got to lay over here for a spell anyway to let the cattle git back in shape."

Since that day at the Rio Grande, when Clay had saved the life of the squatty, flat-nosed, taciturn man, Q had done his work phlegmatically, without complaint. He had proved to be an average trail hand, obviously experienced in handling cattle, but also obviously not interested in that occupation as a way of life. The other members of the crew avoided him. It wasn't that they were afraid of him. Young or old, creaky or not, the Patchsaddle riders were beginning to be afraid of nothing. They were firming into a hard-core unit that had an unspoken objective. They meant to put this herd through to the finish, or die in the attempt. And there was no doubt in the minds of any that more of them would likely die before they saw the end of this trail.

They steered clear of Q mainly because they didn't want to intrude. He always slept with his rifle, his six-shooter, his hiding knife within quick reach of his bed. He was the only one who never talked of his past, or his future. In fact he did not talk at all, except on matters in connection with the welfare of the cattle. It was taken for granted that he was an outlaw. Because of his hard-case appearance, the others could not believe that Q was paying out a debt. Only Clay was certain of that. Q was with the drive because of an unshakable belief that he must repay Clay for saving his life.

"Care to tell me where you figure to find these men?" Clay asked.

"Hackberry, maybe," Q said. "It's a piece west o' here. Not too far, but it might take a little time to look up the boys I have in mind."

Clay had heard of Hackberry, and its reputation. It was headquarters for buffalo hunters and Indian traders, and a haven for outlaws.

"You seem to be acquainted in these parts," Clay said.

"I've been around," Q said, shrugging.

Rose Lansing was listening. She was wearing her apron, and there was flour on her hands. She had been mixing sourdough-biscuit batter in the top of a sack of flour. The Dutch oven stood heating on the wood coals. Clay did not dare look in her direction, for he could picture her expression of disapproval.

"If you find these boys," he told Q, "let them know that all we can pay is twenty-five a month and grub, with maybe a little sweetening of the pot if we get through to end of steel without losing many head. Make sure they understand one other thing. We don't help fight off posses or reward hunters."

Q displayed one of his rare, twisted grins. "I'll tell 'em."

"Got any money?" Clay asked. When Q shrugged, he turned to Rose Lansing. "Give him a ten-dollar piece out of the fund," he said. "He's got to eat and buy fodder for his horse."

She held her nose high, but disappeared around the wagon and presently returned with a gold piece which she gave to Clay who turned it over to Q. It came from the dwindling expense fund that remained from the mortgage money she had received.

She did not speak until after Q had saddled a fresh horse and had ridden away. "So now we're going to hire more outlaws," she said grimly.

"Our job," Clay said, "is to get these cattle to market."

She walked away, stiff-backed, to join Rachel at the cooking duties. Her sense of guilt was bearing heavier on her each day.

Clay watched Q vanish into the country westward. There was no doubt in his mind that this was dangerous ground for Q and that he was unquestionably taking a risk in showing himself in Hackberry, where he evidently was known, and where there might be Rangers or other law officers. This was one of Q's ways of paying off the obligation he believed he owed Clay.

He and the remainder of the Patchsaddle crew settled down to wait. The dry drive had taken forty or fifty pounds off every animal, Clay estimated, but after a few days on water and forage he could see the wrinkles vanishing from their hides.

The men too had thinned, but the efforts of Rose Lansing and Rachel at the cook fires took care of that. Clay did not realize that he might have lost more than the others until he became aware that Rose Lansing and Rachel were favoring him with extra tidbits, and standing by aggressively to see that he ate them.

"I declare!" Rachel said in despair. "I never did see a human what was harder for to take on tallow. This here man is an insult to our cookin', Missus Lansing. Look at that Micah man of mine. He's fattenin' up like a shoat in a harvest field, but this one only gits narrower. He *worries* it off."

Four days passed. Five. The cattle were recovered now, and ready to be thrown on the trail again. But no word came back from Q.

"You'll never see that man again," Rose Lansing said,

almost hopefully. "I couldn't blame him. I must say anybody would be a fool to come back to this ragtag outfit."

"He'll come back if he can," Clay said.

She sighed. "Yes," she said. "You're right. He's a strange one. He believes in paying off a debt."

Clay continued to hold the herd, concealing his burning impatience. For one thing, he could not move the herd ahead with this skeleton crew. But he had faith in Q. He believed the man would return if he was alive and free. But he might be dead, or in some sheriff's jail.

Riders appeared late in the afternoon of the sixth day. None among them was Q. As they came closer Clay made out a badge on the vest of the burly-chested, red-bearded man who rode in the lead.

"A posse, or I never seed one," Micah said.

Micah was correct. The posse rode up, and all the members dismounted without awaiting the customary invitation to alight. There were six of them, all saddle-weary, dusty, hungry, and palpably in no mood for idle talk. All were exceedingly heavily armed.

The big man glared belligerently around. His lips were cracked; his large nose was peeling from windburn. Alkali dust had whitened his stiff stubble of beard.

"What in hell do you call this outfit?" he demanded.

Ann Lansing answered that before Clay could speak. "And who in the hell is asking?"

That rocked the officer back on his heels. He peered closer, then took a second look and a third. He gazed at Rachel, then at Cindy, then at Rose Lansing. He blinked owlishly. He fumbled for the brim of his hat and removed it.

"I'm sorry, ma'am," he mumbled. "Didn't know there was ladies present. I'm Deputy Sheriff Sim Kimball from Hackberry. And you might be Missus—Missus—?"

"The name is Miss Lansing," Ann said crisply. "We would ask you to dismount, but it seems you've already done so."

Sim Kimball had lost the initiative. He tried to regain it. He glared officiously around. He studied Beaverslide Smith, who, at the moment, was trying to mend the heel of one of his worn short boots, using the shoe last that was carried in the supply wagon. Beaverslide's yellowish bald head glinted in the sun. His puckered old eyes were gazing at the visitors with disdain. "They never did teach 'em manners up here in no'th Texas," he observed scathingly.

Kimball's attention turned to Parson Jones, who was washing his socks in the creek. His gaze swung to Ham Marsh and his tubby stomach, who was endeavoring to repair his old saddle, which had suffered some new disaster. Then to Lonnie Randall, who was wearing a pair of his father's oversize breeches and shirt.

Kimball looked at his possemen to make sure they were seeing the same sights. They were staring, bug-eyed. Kimball wagged his head as though still not believing it.

"We been ridin' three days, an' maybe four," he said. "I ain't quite sure of it. I ain't sure of nothin' anymore. It makes a man a little testy. Who's roddin' this here outfit?"

"I am," Clay said. "This is a mixed herd out of San Dimas down below the Nueces. We're bound for market in Missouri."

"Missouri? You mean you figure you can really?—I mean how soon do you aim to git there?"

"We'll make it," Clay said. "What's on your mind, Deputy?"

Kimball produced a much-creased paper from his pocket, carefully unfolded it, for it was about to fall apart. It proved to be a poster of the kind put out for wanted men, to be posted in railway stations and law offices. The subject of this particular dodger, according to the black-type headline, was wanted for bank robbery. A picture was printed, along with a detailed description. The name of the wanted man was listed as Kirby Kane. The picture was smudged and had been taken years earlier, but there was no doubt as to Kirby Kane's identity. He and Q were one and the same.

"Ever seen this feller before?" Kimball asked.

Ann Lansing had moved to peer over Clay's shoulder. He knew she was about to speak, and believed she was going to deny any such knowledge, but he got there first.

"Maybe," he said.

He heard her draw an angry sigh. She had expected him to lie.

Sim Kimball was enlivened. "Where? When?"

"Three, four weeks ago," Clay said. "Down on the Rio Grande. We were taking delivery of that big jag of reds you see in the herd. A fellow who looked like this one was working with the *vaqueros* under a rancher named Pedro Sanchez."

Kimball's burst of hope faded. He sagged back into apathy. "In Mexico?" he moaned. "Weeks ago? What good will that do me now? He was up here in Hackberry only a few days ago, an' shore raised hell, shoved a chunk under it, an' left it tilted."

"My goodness!" Ann Lansing cried. "What did he do?"

"What didn't he do? He's wanted for kidnapin', mayhem, unlawful entry, torture, an' half a dozen other items that they'll git around to after they ketch him, not to mention stickin' up a bank."

It was Clay's turn to be a trifle staggered. "How could he do all that way up here when I saw him in Mexico?" he asked.

"Mexico ain't so fur away he couldn't git here ahead of a bunch of cow critters in four weeks' time," Kimball said. "Not satisfied with havin' nigh ruined pore old Jonathan Pickens by robbin' his bank a year or so ago, he rides into Hackberry a few nights ago, busts into Jonathan's house, marches him out, an' rides away with him. We find Jonathan the next day, tarred an' feathered, an' tied to a tree with the sign of the double cross dabbed on his chest."

"This fellow on this law dodger did all this?" Clay asked incredulously. "This Kirby Kane?"

"He had help. Jonathan allowed there must have been four or five more in on it. But he was blindfolded, an' all he heard was voices an' footsteps and the horses when they rode away."

Clay was nonplussed. It sounded fantastic. Rose Lansing spoke. "I can round up a bait of food for you men. I know you're in a hurry, so I'll have to serve it cold. Leftover cornbread and meat from the pot. I'll open some tomatoes and peaches. It will be filling at least. It's a long ride to Mexico."

"Mexico?" Kimball echoed, wincing.

"This man you're looking for came from there," Rose said. "Where else would he be heading for after committing all those awful crimes? How much of a start did he have on you men?"

One of Kimball's posse spoke. "Damned if I'm headin' for Mexico, Sim, beggin' your pardon, ma'am, for the slip of the tongue. I've had enough. This feller didn't actually hurt that old skinflint anyway. Just tarred an' feathered him up a leetle. There's a lot o' folks around here who figure that Jonathan was overdue for it."

Other men in the posse voiced firm support of that viewpoint, both as having no desire to proceed to Mexico and as to the nature of Jonathan Pickens' character. Sim Kimball was plainly glad to be ruled by majority opinion. "We accept your offer, ma'am," he said gallantly, and became affable, now that he saw a graceful way to escape from a futile pursuit.

Clay faded into the background while Rachel and Rose, with Ann's help, fed the possemen. Finally Ann joined him. "You got out of that gracefully and without telling an actual fib," she said. "I always knew the Burnets were accomplished at slippery doings. What in the world was on Q's mind, do you suppose? Did he go loco?"

"I doubt that," Clay said.

"We'll never see him again, of course," she said.

"We'll see him."

"Why are you so sure?"

"Because of that notion he carries that he owes it to me to see this drive through and watch over me. He'll show up."

"But if he doesn't what will we do?"

"Hit the trail. What else?"

"With this crew? That's impossible!"

"I never thought it was possible that I'd be standing here talking to a Lansing, and driving Lansing cattle to market," Clay said. "But here we are. Anything's possible after that. We'll hang around a while longer. I still think we'll hear from him."

He was right. But it was not until after dark more than twenty-four hours later, and the confidence he outwardly exhibited was beginning to wear thin, when Q returned. He was sitting apart from the wagon, a tin cup of coffee in his hand, when he heard a low, cautious whistle from the background. He arose and located the whistler. It was Q, or Kirby Kane, as he was named on the law dodger.

"Have they gone?" Q whispered. "The posse?"

"Long ago," Clay said. "Yesterday afternoon. They were heading back to Hackberry and glad of it. They'd had enough. We sort of pushed them into believing you were on your way to Mexico, and that they didn't have a chance of catching you. Fact is, I got the idea that some of them weren't too much interested in catching up with you anyway."

Q chuckled. "Jonathan Pickens ain't exactly the most popular citizen in Hackberry."

He uttered a low whistle. There was movement in the darkness. Several men, leading saddled horses, presently came out of the shadows.

"Here are some fellers who are lookin' for ridin' jobs," Q said. "Some of 'em has worked as trail hands, an' you'll find 'em worth their pay. One or two might need a leetle proddin', bein' as they was born lazy, but they'll stick with us if things get touchy."

Clay eyed Q's companions. Rose Lansing and her daughter, attracted by the sound of voices, left the campfire and came walking to join him. They also peered in silence.

Rose Lansing finally spoke. "Heaven help us!"

Q had brought five men with him. The glow of the wagon fire faintly reached them. Two were wearing knee-length black coats in the plantation style, along with ruffled shirts and stocks, all frayed and threadbare. Clay tabbed them as tinhorn gamblers at best. One was rail-thin and over six feet, the other short-coupled, with a wide mouth. Two others wore brush jackets, foxed breeches, and cowboots, garb that was also far from new. The fifth had on a blanket jacket, checked shirt, striped pantaloons that were stuffed into knee-high Conestoga boots, and a round pancake felt hat. A bullwhacker's garb. Still, he did not exactly stack up in Clay's eyes as a man who followed that arduous and dangerous profession regularly.

They were of different sizes, different faces, different dress, but all had one trait in common. They were young, hard-bitten, reckless, with a go-to-hell set to their mouths and their postures.

"This one here goes by the name of Zeno," Q said. "We call him Z for short." He was indicating the bullwhacker.

"And I take it that these others are known as A, B, C and D?" Rose Lansing spoke caustically.

"Now how did you guess it?" Q responded.

Rose Lansing clapped a hand to her forehead in despair. "If you think for one minute we intend to—"

"The pay's twenty-five a month and found," Clay said. "Is that satisfactory to you men."

"Provided the grub is what Kir—I mean Q here—says it is," one of the cowboys said. "He tells me you git real home cookin' with this outfit. Female cookin'."

"Best fodder any trail crew ever had," Clay said. "But, if you throw in with us, you're to stick all the way. Our destination is a railroad somewhere in the state of Missouri. That means crossing the Indian country."

"Do you think I'm going to stand for traveling with these men?" Rose Lansing moaned. "Why—why, they're nothing but a pack of out—"

Her daughter spoke hastily. "Mother, you're taking the wrong view. They look like righteous, upstanding men to me."

"How can you say that?" her mother groaned. "We know they just tarred and feathered some poor man there in this Hackberry place, and are wanted by the law for that and heaven knows what else."

"We didn't really tar that old buzzard," the tall tinhorn said. "All we did was smear some axle grease on him an' dust him with cockleburs."

"We couldn't find no tar," the smaller tinhorn explained. "So we had to use whatever was handy."

Q spoke to Clay. "You can call me Kirby. I reckon the law man told you that was my name."

"We'll continue to call you Q," Clay said. "As far as we're concerned, you've never had any other name."

"Thanks," Q said. "But, so that we don't get the alphabet mixed up, maybe we better call some of these others by name. The tall one, dressed like an undertaker, is Bass. The short-coupled one is Ace. Them two there are Cass an' Des. You've already met Zeno. Clear enough?"

"Clear as a hole in a patch of quicksand," Clay said. "We'll get them straightened out in time. I take it that Ace and Bass aren't really undertakers. My guess is that they're better at burying dead hands in the discard than burying the real thing."

Q grinned. "You could be right. Don't get into any poker games with 'em. Nor with Zeno either. He ain't exactly as stupid as he looks."

"How about you two?" Clay asked the pair who called themselves Cass and Des. "What's your speciality?"

"Punchin' cattle," Cass said with an injured expression. "What else."

"I wouldn't want to guess," Clay said. "I'll cut saddle strings to all of you in the morning. The herd's rested and snorting to hit the trail. We'll string out at daybreak."

"We got clothes in our war sacks that will do better than what we got on," Ace said. "We better camp out in the brush tonight. No use crowdin' in on you folks right away."

Clay understood that Ace and his friends did not want to take a chance that Sim Kimball and the posse might decide to make a return visit.

Rachel, who had been listening, spoke. "See to it dat you stay dar. I'm goin' to sleep mighty light, an' I'll have a butcher knife under my pillow, I tell you. I don't cotton to havin' bank robbers an' such wanderin' around my bed."

"Be quiet!" Micah rumbled angrily. "Dese men come here to help us."

"To cut our throats, most likely," Rose Lansing said.

"Don't listen to her," Ann Lansing said. "I want you to know we appreciate your coming here to help us."

"An' we ain't bank robbers either," Ace, the short-coupled tinhorn said, injured. "Kir—I mean Q here—got double-crossed by that old miser, Jonathan Pickens. He's charged with a whizzer that ol' Jonathan pulled for his own profit."

"Do tell us more," Rose Lansing said with tart skepticism.

"You wouldn't believe us anyway, ma'am." Q spoke mildly. "You've got your mind set ag'in us. Anyway, we're sort o' weary. We been dodgin' that posse for days."

Clay walked with the six men as they retreated from reach of the firelight. Q had given him a glance that indicated he had more to say, but wanted to say it away from the ears of others.

Reaching the brush, and inspecting what they carried

on their horses, he discovered that the newcomers lacked bedding of any kind, and intended to make the best of it for the night, as they evidently had been doing during their flight. He realized they probably had little or nothing to eat recently.

He returned to camp to speak with Rachel and Rose Lansing. They responded with speed, if not with enthusiasm, by pitching in to prepare a second meal. Clay rounded up tarps and what spare blankets he could find, and carried them into the brush where Q and his men were waiting, smoking pipes and cigarettes.

When the food was brought on tin plates by the women, the six men fell to with appetites that aroused comment from Rachel. "I declare, if they're gonna stow away provisions like that, we'll git to Missoury with nothin' but hides an' bones. They'll eat de whole herd."

"Don't worry, gal," Zeno said with a wide, friendly grin. "As a rule we don't eat our own beef. We got a tooth for slow elk."

"Dat's one thing I kin believe," Rachel said. "An' dis slow elk wears brands, I take it. Other folks' brands."

After the women had returned to the wagons, Clay looked around at the shadowy figures. "Do you want to tell me anything?" he asked. "You know our side of it. We're driving cattle to market. That's enough to keep us busy. We don't hanker to take on any side lines."

"Such as robbin' banks?" Ace asked tersely.

"That's right," Clay said. "That's what I want made clear."

Q spoke. "This is the way it is, whether you will believe it nor not. About a year ago Jonathan Pickens run a high blaze on me. I was hangin' out in Hackberry, doin' this an' that, mainly buffalo huntin', pickin' up jobs with cow outfits, an' with freight outfits. Even drove stagecoach for a while. The country is full of fellers like me who'd fought in the war, an' was jest driftin' around, tryin' to keep body an' soul together, like me an' my brothers an' cousins here."

"Brothers? Cousins?"

"These two shorthorns that look like tinhorns are my brothers," Q said. "Ace is older than me, an' Bass younger. Cass an' Des are first cousins. Their paw and my paw were brothers. We're a sort of clannish family. Root stock in Georgia. We cling together. When a feller does dirt to one of us he sorta takes on all of us in a bundle."

"What about this one?" Clay asked, indicating Zeno.

"No relation," Q said, grinning. "Just a friend what sorta speaks our language. An' a bluebelly at that. He fought ag'in us. Now we're pals."

"You're referring to this Jonathan Pickens as the one who did you dirt, I take it?" Clay observed.

"Us six had scraped together enough to start a little brand of our own a few miles out of Hackberry," Q said. "We figure that the buffalo will soon be thinned out an' that cattle might be worth somethin' if you could hang and rattle long enough. Jonathan Pickens owned the bank in Hackberry. It wasn't much of a bank, o' course, but Jonathan had a way of talkin' big, walkin' big, an' impressin' folks. Wore a stovepipe hat, quoted the Bible, an' was a real buttermouth. He also liked to play poker, a habit no banker ought to indulge in. He was a bad poker player, but he believed he was a cyclone on the plains when it come to playin' cards. He got to owin' quite a few folks. It was money he didn't own, of course, but nobody knew just how poor off the bank really was. I finished two hundred dollars ahead of him in a stud game one evenin'. He said he didn't have the money on him, but asked me to go over to the bank where he'd git it from his private safe."

"My brother was a danged fool," Bass said. "He might have knowed Jonathan had somethin' up his sleeve."

"I'd had a few drinks an' was happy," Q said, sighing. "It was near midnight. I went to the bank with him, waited while he fumbled around in his office. He gave me the money, an' I rode on back to the ranch, callin' it a night.

"I was woke up about midmornin'. It was Bass here, tellin' me to hit the trail. Seems like they'd found Jonathan Pickens hog-tied an' gagged in the bank, the big safe busted wide open with a sledgehammer, an' all the bank's money gone. Jonathan allowed that I was the one who'd done it an' had scooted away. It seems that I was supposed to have got away with more'n ten thousand dollars, which busted the bank an' cost the depositors everything they'd put into the place. O' course, it was what Jonathan had stole from the safe that night, cached it, then come back, tied hisself up an' waited until he was found the next mornin' so he could accuse me."

Q paused a moment, then said dryly. "I was mighty sure they'd believe Jonathan rather than me or my brothers. We wasn't exactly what you'd call leading citizens. Maybe we had sold a few cattle that we didn't have sales receipts for, an' maybe some of us had run in a cold deck at times in poker games. But we never really hurt nobody. Even fellers like us have to eat when our bellies pinch our backbones. So I lit out for Mexico on a fresh horse that Bass had ready for me."

"And the rest of you have been hanging around Hackberry ever since?" Clay asked. "Why?"

"Wal," Ace explained. "In the first place we didn't take kindly to bein' swindled. Our little cowspread was took over when they liquidated what assets the bank had after Jonathan hid the cash. We'd borrowed from the bank to buy the water rights. At ten per cent. Jonathan bought himself a good ranch, which included our place, pretendin' he'd borrowed the money from a brother back east. So we figured he owed us a living, an' stayed on."

"Living?"

"Jonathan's beef tasted better than anything else we could think of," Ace said modestly. "An' didn't cost anything. Jonathan knew we was slow-elkin' him, an' tried every way he could think of to ketch us. I reckon he might have succeeded in time. But we sort of enjoyed seein' him stomp and froth. We knew we had about run out our string when Kirby showed up an' told us about a man he admired who needed a little help on the trail. We had a few drinks, an' as a partin' gesture, rode over to Jonathan's ranch an' greased him up some. He's likely got it all swabbed off by this time."

"You're all hired," Clay said. "We'll be across the Red and out of Texas in less than a week with luck. Until then you'll have to keep your eyes peeled for law men."

"There's another little matter," Q said. "I bumped into a man you know in Hackberry. It was Bill Conners, the feller you fired down the trail."

"In Hackberry?" Clay responded. "You must be mistaken. Conners is back in the San Dimas, a long way south by this time."

"No mistake," Q said. "It was Conners. He's sort of gone maverick. He hangs out with a tough bunch whose speciality is stampeding herds in order to rustle strays. They also stick up a stagecoach or so now and then. An' Conners is figurin' on doin' a little more stampeding of a certain cattle drive ag'in which he packs a grudge."

Clay came to taut attention. "Say that again."

"It wasn't the whirligig that pore little darkie girl had made, an' for which she blames herself because that cowboy got killed that day. It was Conners who spooked the herd. He sneaked up a gully on the flank where there wasn't anybody in sight, waved a blanket in the faces of some animals that was grazin', an' that did it. It just happened, by bad luck, that little Cindy had started her whirligig on the far side of the bedgrounds at the same time."

"How do you know this?"

"Conners showed up in Hackberry nigh onto two weeks ago. Cass an' Zeno got into some poker games with him. No big stakes, o' course, but just to pass the time. Conners wasn't much of a poker player, an' he couldn't carry his likker either. He'd heard that Cass an' Zeno had reps as hard noses, an' he wanted to build himself up. He got to talkin' about how tough he was. He did some whisky talk one night about how he'd stampeded a herd which was bossed by a feller he didn't like. Said he'd been headin' north waitin' a chance to repeat the trick until that herd was wiped out or so spoiled nobody could drive it. He was waitin' in Hackberry 'til this herd come on up the trail."

Clay didn't speak for a long time. "This will be mighty good news to Cindy," he finally said. "She's been heart-broken. Maybe she'll start smiling again. She's been breaking my own heart with those sad eyes."

"Mine too," Q said. "How are you goin' to make her believe it? She'll figure that you're making it up."

"You'll see," Clay said. "How far away is this Hack-berry?"

"Four, five hours ride."

"Where would a man be likely to run across Bill Conners there?"

Q stared closer at Clay in the darkness. "Now wait a—"

"Where?"

"You know that I can't go in with you," Q said slowly. "Nor any of us. Sim Kimball would throw us in jail an' lose the key."

"Where?" Clay repeated.

"If he's still there he'll likely spend part of the evenin' at a saloon hangout called Hunter's Rest," Cass spoke.

"Did Conners see you, Q?" Clay asked.

"No," Q said. "It was Cass an' Zeno what had anything to do with him. I spotted him a few times, but kept out of his way, once I'd made sure it was really him."

CHAPTER 8

Pale smoke from the juniper firewood laid a fragrant haze in the morning air as the crew ate breakfast, mingling with the aroma of frying meat, of cornbread, of coffee. The herd grazed quietly in the distance on a rolling prairie. The breaks of the Double Mountain Fork stood purple and peaceful to the northeast. The sun had not yet pushed its golden eye over the rim of the land.

"A mornin' like this makes a man forgit thar's sich things as saddleburs, night guard, an' buffalo gnats," Parson Jones said, finishing off a slab of cornbread, sweetened with sirup. "There's days when the Lord is more'n good to us."

Tiny Cindy Stone was standing, with widening brown eyes, watching Clay. He sat by the supply wagon with a stiff square of paper in his hands. It was a sheet from a calendar advertising a railroad, the same material with which Cindy's mother had fashioned the whirligig the day of the stampede in which Tom Gary had died.

Clay was shaping another whirligig. He completed the toy. Pinning its center with a sliver of cottonwood that he had whittled, he fixed it to a small stick.

"No!" Cindy suddenly sobbed. "No!"

Ann Lansing turned from the iron cook pot where she had been helping her mother and Rachel and became aware of what was going on. A spatula still in her hand, she came walking to stand beside the terrified Cindy. She did not speak as Clay got to his feet and held the toy aloft so that it caught the morning breeze.

"Don't!" Cindy screamed. "Please!"

The whirligig began to spin nicely. Clay moved to Cindy, took her hand. She hung back in terror, but he said, "Cattle aren't afraid of these things, darling. We were wrong that day. It was something else that started the stampede. A bad man who was hiding on the other side of the bedground scared the cattle into running."

He and Cindy moved toward the cattle as he held the spinning whirligig aloft. He could feel Cindy's small fingers gripping tighter and tighter. He was taut inside. Cattle were unpredictable. Bill Conners could have been boasting.

But the cattle were paying no heed. A few raised their heads from grazing, staring with bovine indifference, then returned to foraging.

Clay laughed. "See!" he exclaimed. "It's not scaring them now, and it didn't scare them that day." He swung Cindy up on his shoulder, placed the toy in her hand and walked back to the wagon. "Tomorrow," he said, "I'll make you a paper arrow that will sail on the wind."

Cindy began to smile. It was only a feeble, tremulous smile at first, but it slowly blossomed. Cindy's young mind was free again, her heart lighter.

He walked to where Lonnie Randall had driven the *remuda* into the rope corral. He cut out the mount he wanted, roped it, saddled it, and thrust a rifle in the sling. He buckled on his six-shooter and mounted the horse.

"I'll be gone a day or two maybe," he said. "I'll pick up the herd along the way. Jess, you rod the drive until I get back."

Jess Randall, the man he was placing in charge, stood dumbfounded. "But—" he began to stammer.

"I've got a little business to attend to," Clay said. "Personal business."

Rose Lansing and her daughter became aware that he was leaving and came hurrying, questions on their lips. He did not look at them, but rode away. Jess Randall had proved to be a levelheaded, capable man. The weather was mild, and according to Clay's information conditions were ideal for driving cattle for the next seventy or eighty miles to Red River.

He headed west. Hackberry lay in that direction. He took his time, throwing off at noon for a leisurely nap in the shade of brush along a small stream. He again let the horse set its own pace. The sun was casting long shadows back of him when he sighted the haze of smoke that marked the location of the settlement. He dallied again, resting alongside a sizable stream above the town until twilight settled.

Mounting, he rode into Hackberry. It was an unplanned scatter of nondescript structures, some built of sod or stone, others of adobe or logs. It stood at a stagecoach crosstrail and was the last jumping-off place for the Indian and buffalo country. It served as a supply point for the Army, and for cattlemen, and had attracted a population of perhaps two thousand persons, Clay estimated.

The principal street meandered aimlessly. The mud of spring had dissolved into gritty dust under a summer sun that blew in blinding curtains from the churning wheels of passing freight wagons. Bull-team, mule, and horse freightyards fringed the settlement, and the air was foul with the stench of buffalo hides that were stacked in great ricks, awaiting transport north. Livestock grazed by the hundreds in corrals and feedyards around the town.

More than half of the establishments were gambling houses or saloons. Some were shacks of sheetiron and mud, with plank bars set on sawhorses and candles for light. These catered to the besotted, the penniless, the vicious.

Higher up on the scale were emporiums which had mirrored backbars and gambling layouts that included roulette tables and birdcage games. At least two of these sported small stages with velvet curtains where entertainment would be offered during the evening.

The name painted across the false front of the largest of these places was the one Clay was seeking.

Hunter's Rest,

Mort Quinn, Prop.

Clay rode slowly past Hunter's Rest, glancing over the top of the slatted swing doors. He gained a partial view of the interior. There were only four or five patrons at the bar at this early hour. One poker table was in operation with four men holding cards. He saw no sign of the person he was hunting.

He found an eating place, tied up his horse at the front where he could keep an eye on it through the window, and entered.

Soldiers, buffalo hunters, bullwackers, men of uncertain callings occupied the tables. Eyes turned briefly toward him as he stood his rifle in a wall rack along with other such weapons, and selected a space on a bench at a table. They took in the holster gun, measured his height, his garb, his boots, which classified him as a trail man. They lost interest in him, and returned to the business of eating as much food as possible in the time allotted.

A tin plate was slapped in front of him, along with a mug for coffee. "Gimme a dollar, mister, an' eat yore fill," the waiter snarled. "Then make room fer others."

The food was served in huge platters and bowls, which sprouted big iron forks and spoons. It was solid, and filling—and heavy with grease. Clay helped himself but only pretended to be hungry. He sized up all who were leaving the place, trying to determine if they might have recognized him and were on their way to carry the news to someone. He found no such evidence.

He finished eating, and strolled into the full darkness of the town. He led his horse to a livery, paid another dollar for stall and board. The animal would be reasonably safe from theft in the livery. He cased the town which was now growing livelier as the evening advanced. Women stood in doors beckoning. Barkers appeared in front of dance halls, bellowing the advantages of the establishments where there were percentage girls, entertainment, and crooked gambling tables, no doubt.

He passed a building which was now a saddlery and leather shop, but on whose walls, beneath a coat of white-wash, could still be made out a printed sign which identified it as the past location of the Hackberry Safety Bank, Jonathan Pickens, Prop. Farther on, a new bank, with new names in gilt paint, had taken the place of the bankrupt establishment.

Clay finally returned to Hunter's Rest. It was a sizable place as such things went. It had originally been built in the slat-length style, but business had been so rushing that an addition had been added in a wing at the side to accommodate the gambling layouts.

He moved to the bar, taking a position where the light from the lamps did not reach him directly. He ordered a beer, which came in a mug, mainly foam and not too cold.

Bill Conners was not in the place, which was growing increasingly busy. All the tables were in operation, and the bar was lined with men drinking, smoking, and yarning. A piano player began tinkling out a tune near the curtained stage.

Clay had ordered his second beer when Bill Conners came through the swing doors into the place. He was accompanied by two men. Conners had changed in the weeks since he had parted from the Patchsaddle crew. As range boss at the Lansing ranch, he had been somewhat of a dandy, dressing with a flash and a flair, a frequent visitor to the Jackville barbers and clothing stores.

Evidently he was now drinking hard. His white shirt was soiled, his features had thickened, and his eyes were bloodshot. A fold of flesh overlapped his belt. He packed a brace of six-shooters, whose handles jutted big and clumsily from his sides. In the past he had never posed as a gunman, preferring to depend on his reputation as a pugilist to awe lesser men.

He moved to the bar, shouldering aside patrons who happened to be in his way. "The red stuff, Al!" he called to the bartender, who was busy with a group of customers. "*Pronto!* I'm thirsty. Where's Gloria?"

"She'll be around," the barkeeper responded. "She's never this early. You know that. She don't sing till nine o'clock."

Clay sized up Conners' companions. One was a puffy, alcohol-soaked man who had the earmarks of a thug who would cut a throat for a dollar. The other was young, cotton-haired, with thick lips, coarse features, and the vacuous smile of a child. Both he and the puffy one packed six-shooters in holsters. Clay decided they were the kind who had knives, sheathed in handy hideouts, which they preferred to use. Of the two, he rated the cotton-haired one as the more dangerous. This one was brainless, heedless, with no conscience, no future, no past.

Clay moved into the nearest circle of lamplight. Bill Conners sloshed whisky into a glass, raised the glass, then stood in that attitude, peering.

"It's really me, Bill," Clay said. "Imagine finding me here. And you also. You really should have gone back to the San Dimas."

Conners carefully placed the untasted glass back on the bar. "What's on your mind, Burnet?" he asked.

"One or two things," Clay said. "One concerns Tom Gary. His best friends wouldn't have known him after that stampede went over him that morning down the trail. But we all knew him anyway, and gave him Christian burial."

"I don't know what you're talking about," Conners said.

Conners' two companions were standing open-mouthed, taken by surprise. Clay spoke to them. "Stay out of this. It's between me and this leppie here. He stampeded my herd a while back. One of my crew was ground to mincemeat under the hoofs. I happen to know that he has bragged that he aims to stampede me again and again."

Around them, men began backing hastily away, looking for cover. The alarm spread to the gambling tables. Play stopped, faces were staring, startled.

"Don't try to draw," Clay said. "I don't want to have to kill you. I figure you're going to live with Tom Gary's ghost the rest of your life, and that's what you deserve. You knew Tom Gary, you were even a friend of his. I came here to beat you with fists, and to let you know that if you ever come near a drive of mine again I'll do it over and over again until you'll look worse than poor Tom Gary did when we found him that day."

He added, "Take off all that iron that's hanging on you. It won't be of any help to you now. You're no gunman, anyway, only a false front."

A pudgy man with a paste diamond in his necktie, appeared back of the bar with a double-barreled buckshot gun in his hands. "Take it outside, boys," he said. "I own this place, and I don't want it wrecked."

"More light in here," Clay said. "And this won't take long."

He moved in, yanked the guns from Conners' holsters, and slid them out of reach down the bar. He handed his own pistol over to the saloon man.

Conners was thirty pounds heavier. He had not wanted a gunfight with Clay, but he was now eager, for this was in his element. He thirsted to maim and maul the man to satisfy the hatred that had darkened his life. He charged in greedily. Clay moved inside the arc of Conners' blows and they lost power, expending themselves harmlessly on his shoulders. He drove punches to Conners' stomach, and heard the rush of agony from lungs. He took a smash to the jaw that had stunning force. He weathered that and again delivered punishment to the body.

Conners reeled back. He braced himself against the bar

and caught Clay to the forehead with a sledging right, then a left to the chin that sent Clay staggering back against a table. Conners rushed in to finish the fight. Clay caught the chair that had been vacated by a poker player and sent it spinning against Conners' shins. Conners was tripped to a hand and knee in the sawdust but lunged to his feet.

Clay met him with punches to the face. Conners' blows suddenly lacked steam. Clay drove a right to the jaw, and then another right. And Conners went down, horrible disbelief in his eyes.

A kicking, fist-mauling, cursing weight landed on Clay's back. It was Conners' young, cotton-haired companion. He was squealing profane, insane promises that he would kill Clay. He was pummeling with both fists, but his own berserk fury was defeating his purpose, and he did little damage.

Clay plunged forward and bucked his new opponent head over heels in a somersault. The cotton-haired one struck a poker table with solid impact. The table was strongly built and withstood the weight. But the cotton-haired was left motionless, the wind knocked out of him.

A gun roared. Clay turned. Conners' second companion, the puffy-eyed one, was standing with a shocked expression on his hard features. A six-shooter was dribbling from the limp fingers of his right hand. It landed in the sawdust. His right arm, which had managed the gun, drooped sickeningly. A bullet had broken his arm midway between elbow and wrist. Blood was appearing.

Powder smoke came spinning past Clay from the bore of a pistol in the hands of a newcomer who had stepped through the swing doors. The arrival was Ann Lansing. She was pale, and palpably horrified by what she had done, but she still held the six-shooter ready to fire again if necessary, her lips set in a tight, determined line.

The place became bedlam, with men diving to cover.

That gradually stilled as no more shooting erupted. Heads began to cautiously appear.

"Come on!" Ann Lansing said to Clay, her voice thin, high-pitched. "Let's get out of here!"

Clay lifted his six-shooter from the hands of the stunned saloon owner and walked to join her. Together they backed through the swing doors—and into the arms of a big man wearing a deputy's badge. Sim Kimball.

"Stand right there!" Kimball thundered. "Turn aroun', while I peel them guns off'n you. Stand quiet, till I say you can move."

Clay looked wryly at Ann Lansing. "Better uncock that gun," he said. "It might go off. You don't want to add shooting a peace officer to your crimes, do you?"

Kimball took their six-shooters and laid them carefully on the ground. He ran his hands over Clay to make sure he had no hideout. He started to do the same with Ann Lansing. There was a sharp report and the deputy staggered back, holding a hand to his face that had been thoroughly slapped.

"Keep your paws off me!" she snapped.

"M'God!" Kimball moaned, continuing to nurse his jaw. "If'n it ain't the pants-wearin' female! An' this other one is thet long-legged boss of that ragged-bottom trail outfit I come across out there. What in blazes are you two doin' startin' a ruckus here in my town?"

Bill Conners, blood crusting his damaged face, came out of the saloon, helping the puffy-eyed man, who was gripping his broken arm and stumbling, dazed by the shock of the injury.

"We got to git a doctor!" Conners snarled. "Gotch, here, has got a bone busted by a slug, an' is bleedin' bad. Them two there done it. Thet gal shot Gotch. Tried to murder him."

"I shot at his arm," Ann Lansing said. "He was the one

who was trying to murder someone. He was going to shoot Clay Burnet in the back."

"Arrest 'em!" Conners demanded.

"Don't neither of you try nothin'," Kimball warned Clay and the girl. "I'll have to take you two into custody till I find out what happened."

A few minutes later Clay and the girl found themselves in the dingy office of a stone-built structure that served as the Hackberry jail. Sim Kimball, with two assistants standing by to watch the prisoners, was laboriously filling out entries in a soiled ledger, and muttering aloud.

"One male, one female, charged with disorderly conduct, attempt to commit murder, resistin' arrest, an—" he mumbled.

"Who resisted?" Ann demanded indignantly.

"—an' assault on a law officer in the performance of his duty," Kimball rumbled ahead.

"My only regret is that I didn't swing harder," she said. "What right did you have to lay hands on me?"

"For all I know you might still have a sneak gun or a pig-sticker cached on you," Kimball said. "You wouldn't let me find out."

"If I had a pigsticker I'd use it," she said.

She glared at Clay. "You are the biggest, conceited fool this side of the River Styx," she said. "Which river you will likely cross before you are much older unless you quit trying to demonstrate how brave you are. You're still trying to prove something, but you're only succeeding in being childish and insufferably heroic. You know you should never have come here alone."

"As long as we're calling names I could think up a few for you," Clay said. "Nobody with an ounce of brains would have followed me here, let alone a rattleheaded girl."

"Somebody had to follow you,'" she said. "I knew you were going to get yourself into hot water."

"How soon do we get out of this sweatbox?" Clay asked Kimball.

The deputy ran a finger over a calendar that hung on the wall. "Three weeks," he said. "Maybe four."

"Three weeks? Maybe four?" Clay and the girl echoed the words in unison.

"Circuit court just closed its session here a few days ago, an' won't be back for a while," Kimball explained. "Then you'll likely be bound over to the grand jury an' taken to the county seat to await trial if you're indicted."

"Good heavens!" Ann Lansing said. "Such a bother. If you think for one minute that I'm going to sit in your filthy jail for weeks, waiting to go through all that rigmarole you're mistaken. Can't we put up bail?"

"That'll have to be set by the judge," Kimball said. "An' from the looks of you two I doubt if you could raise bail, no matter how low it was set. As for sittin' in my jail, which ain't filthy, I want you to know, we don't keep females here. After all, you're a lady even if you don't dress like one. You'll be held at my house. I'm a married man, an' we've got a room all ready fer female prisoners. Last one we had there was a lady who'd kilt her husband with an ax. She's in Huntsville now, life sentence. Should have hung her. My wife's deputized, an' I warn you she kin handle half a dozen yore size, if'n you git any ideas about escapin'."

He looked at Clay. "You'll be held here in this calaboose, an' I don't want no complaints. My jail is the best the county kin afford."

He turned to one of the jailers. "Go fetch Sadie. Tell her we got a prisoner fer her to look after."

After the man had left, Kimball gave Clay and Ann Lansing a wink. "County pays a dollar an' a half a day fer board an' keep when a prisoner is held in special quarters. I don't care if'n the circuit judge never shows up."

Clay and Ann sat on a bench waiting while Kimball again

busied himself at his desk. "You weren't fool enough to have come here alone, were you?" Clay murmured.

"No," she whispered. "I've got a little more sense than one person I could name."

"Who came with you?"

She was reluctant to answer. Finally she said, "My mother."

"Your *mother?* My God! Of all people! Where is she?"

"She waited outside of town while I rode in to scout the situation. Then I got involved. I heard you fighting with Bill Conners in that saloon and looked in in time to see that man trying to shoot you in the back."

"Well at least your mother must know that we're in jail. I hope she has savvy enough to clear out and get back to the wagons before she gets involved too."

The jailer returned, accompanied by Kimball's wife. She was a very broad-beamed, bosomy, muscular woman with an untidy mop of red hair. She wore a brown skirt over many petticoats, a man's saddle jacket on which was pinned a deputy's badge, and had a pistol in a holster strapped around her ample waist.

"Come on, gal," she said, and grasped Ann firmly by the arm. "George tells me you shot up Hunter's Rest tonight an' likely killed a man. It's you smarty, pretty-faces that are always the worst underneath. I'm Deputy Sadie Kimball. You an' me air goin' to git along—if you know what's good for you."

Ann looked back wildly as she was led away. Then the outer door closed behind her. Kimball pushed Clay toward the open door of a cell at the rear. A moment later the door banged shut and a key turned in the lock. Clay was a prisoner in the Hackberry jail. Moths and mosquitos flew freely in and out of the small barred window from which the glass had been removed for ventilation. He heard the dribbling of a rat or lizard in the heavy beams of the roof overhead. He sat down on the bunk which had a thin mattress, evidently stuffed with cornshucks. He was to discover that this was also his chair and table. There was nothing else in the tiny cell.

"There's water, buckets, soap, and mops in the washroom at the back," the turnkey said. He was a wizened, bow-legged man with a sad handle-bar mustache. "We'll tell you when we want to let you out to wash up yourself an' yore cell."

Clay tried to imagine what Rose Lansing might be doing. No doubt she would carry the news back to the trail camp. But what then? He had no answer for that. What could a skeleton crew manned with oldsters like the Parson and Beaverslide do? As for Q and his five companions, they did not even dare show their faces in Hackberry, else they would find themselves in the same predicament as Clay and Ann Lansing. Jailed.

He turned in presently. The turnkey furnished him with a ragged cotton quilt, which was not needed, for the cell was stifling in spite of the open window. He lay wondering about Ann Lansing, about the herd, and about what would happen to it now that he no longer could carry the responsibility.

He slept fitfully. At daybreak he left the bunk and stood with his face pressed to the bars of the window—an opening too small for a man to wriggle through, even if the bars were removed. Hackberry was still asleep at this hour. It awakened slowly, the sun came up. He ate the coarse flapjacks, moistened with molasses, that the jailer brought, along with a cup of water that was tepidly warm.

He returned to his vigil at the window. Hours of it. He had a slanting view into the main street, and his entertainment was the parade of passing freighters, pedestrians, riders, and pack trains. Noon meal was a bowl of stew, prepared by Sim Kimball's wife. Brought from the Kimball home, it was cold by the time it reached him.

The afternoon dragged by, the heat in the cell became a torture. Sundown came and darkness fell, bringing a measure of coolness. He paced his cage, listening to the sounds of conviviality that drifted from the music halls and saloons.

Surely the next day would bring at least some word from Rose Lansing. But the next day passed as monotonously as had the first twenty-four hours. Something must have happened to Rose Lansing.

When twilight came, he furiously rattled the door of his cell until Kimball, who had been cooling himself in a chair on the sidewalk, was forced to take heed. "What's eatin' you?" the deputy demanded.

"I want to see Miss Lansing," Clay snarled.

"What fer?"

"What for? What the hell! So we can find a lawyer who can get her, at least, out of here."

"'Tain' no use. Ain't no lawyer in town now thet court is over. Wouldn't be no use anyway, bein' as both o' you are flat busted. She didn't have a cent on her, Sadie says, an' all you had was little more'n seven dollars. Ain't no lawyer what would be interested in that kind o' money."

Clay gave up the discussion. Another day passed. He again demanded that he be allowed to speak to Ann Lansing. Kimball again refused. "I don't want you two gittin' your haids together to hatch up some deviltry," he said.

A fourth day passed. A fifth day. Clay had the sensation of living in a nightmare. He began to fight the desire to yell and tear at the cell door and the stone walls. He began conjuring all sort of grim theories. They had been deserted. Or, *he* had been deserted. Rose Lansing probably had managed to gain her daughter's release and was on the way north with the drive, leaving him to face the music alone. The feud had been revived.

"You got a visitor," Kimball growled on the afternoon of the sixth day.

The visitor was Ann. She was accompanied by Kimball's buxom wife who stood, arms folded, listening to what was to be said.

Ann came to the cell door. She was thin, drawn, seemed much smaller. "I forced them to bring me here," she said. "I wanted to make sure you were all right."

Clay said weakly, "My God, the things I've been thinking about you. You and your mother. I thought you had—"

"Deserted you? I've been imagining the same thing. Awful things. I believed Sadie Kimball was lying to me, and that you had been turned loose or had escaped. After all, I'm the one who shot that man."

"What's happened?" Clay asked. "Where are they? Why doesn't someone come? Why don't they at least send word?"

"I don't know," she said, fighting back tears. "I just don't know. Clay Burnet, you—you look terrible. Just terrible."

He started to say the same about her, then refrained. Sadie Kimball took her arm, pulled her away. "If'n thet's all you two got to say to each other, then we're all wastin' our time," she said, disappointed. "I figured you two might be sweet on each other."

"Now, whatever made you imagine a thing like that?" Ann said, and wiped away more tears.

"Come on, then," Sadie snapped. "I got a bakin' to do before suppertime."

Clay was again left alone to sweat out the mystery of the apparent desertion of Rose Lansing and the Patchsaddle crew. He knew in his heart it could not be desertion. So he began to picture new wild visions. Something had happened to all of them. Outlaw attack. Rustlers. Indians. They might have been wiped out, the herd stolen.

These demons marched with him. It was sundown again, and he was lying listlessly on the pallet. He suddenly lifted his head, listening. Then he leaped to the window.

"Come to salvation and enlist in the army of the Lord," a deep voice was booming in the street. "Revive your faith in the sacred word of the Testaments, and humble yourself in the knowledge that there will be a Judgment Day."

A hooded wagon creaked into view in the street. On the

seat, booming the message in bell-like tones, was Parson
Ezra Jones. He held the reins of a team of mules in one
hand and brandished the Bible in the other. Stork-thin
and cadaverous, he wore a rusty frock coat, a battered top
hat, a celluloid collar, and a black string tie. Clay recognized
the garments as having once been worn by the tall tinhorn
who called himself Bass. The canvas tilt of the wagon bore
messages, dabbed on in axle grease. "Come To The Lord.
Piety Is The Path To Heaven. Blessed Are The Humble."

The vehicle, which was the Patchsaddle supply wagon,
proceeded out of sight down the street, with the Parson's
voice continuing to roll out the appeal. Along the way,
faces were turning, following the progress of the wagon.
The majority were grinning tolerantly.

Clay waited. He could follow the location of the Parson
by the distant droning of his voice. It became very faint,
then began to strengthen. Soon the wagon reappeared. This
time the Parson swung the team off the street into a vacant
lot alongside the jail.

Sim Kimball, who was smoking a cigar, with his feet on
the desk, was annoyed. "I ought to run that old fanatic
out o' town," he said. "We git one of 'em every month or
so. He'll take up collections 'til he figures he's milked all
the fools dry, spend it on red-eye, then move on to find
another town what will stand for his racket."

It was evident that Kimball had not recognized the Parson
as having been one of the crew at the trail camp he had
visited with the posse. However, he did not follow up his
threat to ostracize the pseudo evangelist, evidently because
that would require effort on a warm day.

The Parson ended his declamation, and began unhitching
his mules and making preparations for what was evidently
to be both an overnight camp and a preaching session.
Clay left the window and returned to the bunk. The Parson
had not once glanced in his direction, but he knew that

he had not been deserted after all, and that action was impending.

He ate the coarse meal that was brought from Sadie Kimball's kitchen, lukewarm, as usual. Darkness settled, and torchlight flared alongside the jail. Parson Jones began preaching, using the wagon seat as a pulpit. A few listeners gathered and more began to drift in. It was a way of passing time. There were catcalls and groans of derision. This brought protests from some of the gathering.

The sermon ended with the collection. Clay heard a few coins clank into a metal object. Then the impromptu revival was over. "Thet old faker will be as drunk as a skunk inside an hour," Sim Kimball predicted. "I shouldn't ever have let him light in this town."

The torch was extinguished. Silence came, as far as the Parson was concerned, although Hackberry was settling down to its nightly round of drinking and gambling. Nine o'clock came, and Sim Kimball locked his desk and headed home, leaving the jail in charge of the turnkey.

Ten o'clock. Midnight. Hackberry was mainly asleep, except for four or five of the gambling traps and music halls. The turnkey was asleep on a cot in the office.

Clay became aware of faint activity outside his window. He heard the snuffling of mules and the creak of harness being adjusted.

A man spoke softly from outside. "Clay, where are you?"

That was Q's voice. Clay moved to the barred window. "Here," he said. "This one." He dangled a hand to mark his location.

Metal clinked. A length of chain was passed through the bars into his hands. It was one of the chains used to lock the wheels of the wagons on steep descents.

"We're goin' to jerk them bars out of their sockets," Q whispered. "Pass the end back to me so I can hook up."

"I doubt if that'll be enough for me to squeeze through," Clay breathed. "This cussed window is child-size."

"I figure part of the wall will go when we give it a yank," Q said. "Stand back. That whole danged jail might come down around your ears. It's only a crackerbox."

Clay stood back. He could hear ropes being attached to the chain. Riders were out there with lariats. The wagon was being backed into position to join in the effort.

"All set," Q said.

"Praise the Lord, an' down go the walls of Jericho!" Parson Jones cried. "Hike!"

His whip cracked. The mules leaped into motion. Clay heard riders grunt as they leaned against saddles to help take up the strain.

Q had judged the strength of the structure correctly. The bars were not only snatched from their seatings, but with them went a section of the stone wall.

Clay leaped through the opening, taking a shower of dust and broken mortar, making it into the clear just as a portion of the roof sagged down, blocking the opening.

The turnkey awakened and began yelling. "This way," Q said. "Don't mind that feller. He cain't git out. We slipped some wedges into the outer door, so he'll be some time gittin' it open."

Clay ran with Q. Riders loomed up. One was Zeno, another Beaverslide Smith. They were cutting away the ropes that had been attached to the wagon, and which had helped breach the walls of Jericho.

The whip cracked again and the wagon took off, swinging through the dark back areas of the town, with Parson Jones handling the reins. Clay was guided at a run to where saddlehorses waited.

"Hold on!" he panted. "Ann Lansing! She's being held at—"

"Here I am," Ann spoke. She was mounted on one of the waiting horses. Clay and Q leaped aboard saddled animals, and they rode away in the wake of the wagon. In addition to Beaverslide and Zeno, he recognized Ham Marsh and Cass as members of the party.

"They got me out first," Ann explained. "It was even easier than wrecking the jail. I was locked in a room, but it was easy to open. Cass, here, seems to have had experience at picking locks. Sadie and Sim Kimball are sound sleepers, especially after they found a bottle of whisky in the kitchen that they didn't know they owned."

There was no sign of immediate pursuit. Clay was sure that would come later when Sim Kimball would have time to organize a posse.

"Take it easy," Q said. "We've got a hundred miles ahead of us, an' we ain't goin' to make it right quick."

"A hundred miles? Where's the herd?"

"The other side of the Red," Q explained. "We forded 'em a couple days ago, then come back to git you two."

"So that's why you let us hang and rattle?" Ann exclaimed wrathfully. "You got the cattle safely out of reach of Texas law before worrying about us. I could have died of anxiety."

"Yore maw figured you'd last it out," Q said complacently. "An' Burnet too. She said you was both young an' tough. Once we got the drive across the Red, we could thumb our noses at Texas badge toters like Sim Kimball. Otherwise he might have clapped a lien on the cattle to hold 'em as security for fines or such."

"Just as I said," Ann Lansing moaned. "My mother thinks more of those blasted cattle than she does of me. She'll never know what I went through with that big ox of a woman, Sadie Kimball. Do you know what Sadie actually asked me?"

"I'm waitin' to hear," Q said.

"She asked me how many other people I had shot during my wicked career."

"And how many is it?" Clay asked.

She glared at him in the starlight. "I might state here

and now," she said, "that the next blasted time you try to act like a big hero, I'll not interfere."

"Amen," Clay said.

"I'll just let you be carried out on a slab!" she cried shrilly. Then, amazingly, she burst into tears.

They overtook the wagon. "Welcome, my children," Ezra Jones said. "We have shattered the walls of Jericho. Now we will wait for the waters of the Red River to part for us."

"I won't count on that," Q said. "I'll just figure on swimmin' it—provided we git there ahead of Sim Kimball. He'll be right red-eared, an' in a mood to do some shootin', after drinkin' that rotgut we left for him, which had the label of good likker, an' after what we done to his jail."

The lights of Hackberry faded back of them. There was still no sign of pursuit, and they slowed the horses. At daybreak they came to where relay horses had been left in a patch of timber, guarded by Des. Food was available. They changed saddles, ate and headed north again, leading the horses they had been riding.

At noon, with seventy miles behind them, they found a second relay of Patchsaddle animals in charge of young Lonnie Randall. Mounted on these fresh mounts and driving with them their augmented *remuda*, they rode on through the afternoon.

At twilight they pushed through scrub pecan, willows, and sycamores into view of Red River. The stream was low, and there was little swimming water to contend with as they crossed, herding their horses, and floating the wagon ahead of them.

The chuck wagon was camped in the fringe of the river brush. The herd was bedded peacefully on open flats of grama and buffalo grass, with Micah and Nate Fuller drowsily singing the cattle to sleep.

Rose Lansing came hurrying to meet them. She took Ann in her arms and wept. "You look thin, darling," she sobbed. "They didn't treat you right, did they? Rachel, fix up a plate for my little girl. And for Clay Burnet too. He's nothing but skin and bones. They've been starving them."

Ann kissed her mother and clung to her. "It's nice to be home," she said, weeping. "Home—and wanted."

Riders appeared in the purple dusk across the river. Clay made out the bulky form of Sim Kimball. The deputy sat there with his posse for a time, shouting threats. Then, defeated, he turned back from the river, and he and his men vanished into the brush.

CHAPTER 9

Clay twisted in the saddle and looked back. The herd
was strung out for nearly half a mile, straggling raggedly
along. Riders slumped hipshot on shambling horses that
bobbed aimlessly along. Bluestem grass was almost stirrup-
high here, but it only added to the suffocating heat of the
summer afternoon.

A man had to turn his face away to parry the lung-
parching aridity of the gusts of wind. Dust devils were
springing into life from the yellow face of a parched stream
bed off to the right. Clay watched the dusters, for one had
built itself into a high, whirling column in sand hills the
previous day, and had come dancing down on the herd,
causing a run that could have been dangerous at another
time, but which had faded away out of the sheer inability of
the cattle to keep going in the heat.

This was the Indian Nations. The blue lacework that were
the Witchita Mountains had faded to the southwest days
ago. Since then the drive had been traveling through a
vacant world, with no horizons to reach, no goals for a
man's future.

No Indian really claimed this land, but all nations
hunted buffalo, deer, wild turkey, and other game that
was as plentiful as the hair on a warrior's scalp. This was
the game paradise of the Pawnee, the Cherokee, the Southern Cheyenne, the Crow, the Comanche, half a dozen other
tribes. Even now, in the heat of midday, Clay glimpsed a
band of deer to the north, and the wind brought the un-
mistakable odor of a great buffalo herd somewhere nearby.

But the great danger now was Indian. Here the tribes-men killed the buffalo that came, they believed, in an end-less river from caverns somewhere far to the south in the Llano Estacado, which white men called the Staked Plains. Here they feasted, made medicine, danced to their gods, fought rival tribes, counted coups, stole women and chil-dren, and lived as free and undisciplined as the wind. They wanted no white man to despoil their paradise.

Every man in the Patchsaddle crew was aware of the possibility of attack. Each morning when they were topping off their first day horses Clay made a point of reminding them to be always on watch. Each night he added an extra man to the shifts on the bedground—an added burden on men who were already in the saddle two thirds of the time.

He wheeled his horse and rode down the flank of the drive. His horse responded listlessly. The riding stock was as dispirited as the men, beaten down by the long days, the monotony, the dust that was always in their nostrils, the heat that never offered mercy, the hot nights that brought the mosquitos, the buffalo gnats, the deerflies.

One rider had strayed wide of his position on the second left swing, mainly to avoid the dust which was being driven his way by the wind in a cloud the color of a shroud. He was Parson Jones.

"Close in, Parson, close in!" Clay shouted. "They're be-ginning to scatter all over hell's acres. If they ever spook they'll explode in all directions and we'll have half The Nations to search. Keep 'em in line."

The Parson obeyed angrily. "That's all I hear," he snarled. "Saddle up! Git movin'. Tighten up them cattle! Eat dust. Eat more dust. If'n I wasn't a God-fearin' man I'd say fer you to go to hell an' take these dem-blasted horns an' hoofs with you."

Clay rode on. The angular, hawk-nosed Parson was in a mood for a real clash. So were all the other members of the crew. Micah, usually the most placid, who accepted hardships as part of life, came charging belligerently up as Clay neared the drag.

"That there feller what calls hisself Cass ain't gittin' along with me none at all," Micah raged. "He's fixed it so I'm always taggin' along with bunch-quitters, an' ridin' my bottom down to the bone. Look at me. I was black dis mawnin'. I'm yella now. Sweat an' dust. I could scrape me off an' build me a 'dobe house. You tell dat Cass man dat—"

"I'll tell him," Clay said hastily. Cass, as a matter of fact, was as dust-caked and in as much of a fighting mood as Micah, from the looks. "Simmer down, you two. There's a lake ahead. Nice cool water. Everybody will have a swim and forget the dust and sweat for a while."

"Lake?" Micah exclaimed. "Ah don't recollect anybody sayin' anything about a lake in dis part o' dis forsaken country."

"Look for yourself," Clay said. "Can't you see the shine of water dead ahead. We'll be there in less than an hour by the looks."

Micah and Cass rose in the stirrups. Then they both climbed onto the saddle standing erect. Their ponies were too jaded to object.

"Glory be!" Cass breathed. "There sure is water ahead. Blue an' cool-lookin'. Water!"

They slid back into the saddles. They were enlivened, suddenly eager. "Watah ahead, boys!" Micah yelled to swing men ahead. "Swimmin' watah! Bathin' watah! Whoopee! We'll be there before sundown."

Cass, whooping, slapped Micah on the back. They both were laughing like idiots. Their bickerings and frustrations were forgotten. They ignored the dust that crusted them and their horses, forgot their hatred of the unpredictable bovines they had been herding for so long. Once more the country looked beautiful to them. They even forgave it for the blistering heat.

The word passed from rider to rider. Wild yells of joy

arose. The tempo changed. Even the horses and the dull-eyed cattle seemed to respond to the lightening spirits of the riders and began stepping ahead faster.

Ann Lansing came riding up to join Clay, her eyes alight. "It's a miracle," she said. "I'm going to ride right into that water, clothes and all."

"Go to the wagons," Clay said. "And stay back. You and all the ladies."

"What do you mean?"

"You'll see."

He circled the herd, speaking to the men. "Better start shedding your duds, boys. No use ruining boots and such. You'll have plenty of time later to do a washing. I'll send the ladies and the wagons off out of sight."

Soon the Patchsaddle drive was traveling ahead through westering sunlight, accompanied by a dozen men clad only in their hats. Clay faded to the rear, then dropped out of sight and joined the women at the wagons.

Rose Lansing, tooling the chuck-wagon team, was standing erect, gazing ahead. The herd was a mile or more to the west. She suddenly glared at Clay. "They'll kill you," she said. "They'll hang you up by your heels—and you deserve it."

Her daughter, who had placed her horse alongside the wagon to profit by its shade, had been peering eagerly ahead also. Suddenly she uttered a gasp. For an instant she went limp in the saddle. Then she snatched up the quirt that hung around the horn and rode toward Clay, swinging the lash aloft.

Her mother snatched the bullwhip from the socket on the dash of the wagon, and sent its length sailing in time to intercept the braided length of the quirt in midair, foiling the girl's blow at Clay.

"No, Ann!" Rose Lansing said. "Wait! It might work. Something had to be done. They were ready to go at each other, tooth and nail. They had to be made to think of something else. Maybe to laugh at themselves. At least to laugh."

"Dar ain't any watah there," Rachel spoke from the seat of the supply wagon. "Mistah Claymore Burnet, you bettah be ready to run fer yore life when dem naked men find out you've made fools of 'em. I can't help laughin'. I'd shore like to see their faces when dey find out dat lake ain't nothin' but a stretch o' dry sand that looks blue, like a mirror under de sky."

Then Rachel began laughing. She laughed harder, rocking back and forth on the seat. Little Cindy joined in. Rose Lansing began chuckling, then burst into uncontrollable laughter. Ann was drawn into the rising hilarity. She draped the whip on the horn, covered her face with her hands, shaking with laughter. It spread to Clay.

In the distance he could see that the point men were becoming aware of the hoax. The nearest was Q. He was standing in the stirrups, craning his neck, staring in disbelief. Clay could visualize the incredulity in Q's tough face, the dawning realization that he had been duped.

Q was also aware that the best way to treat a humbug was to make the best of it. He turned, waving energetically, urging the others forward. They left their places with the jaded cattle and prodded their horses into a gallop.

Clay watched the small, white figures on horseback as they pulled up, far away, staring at the stretch of hot sand that lay across their paths in the sun. They sat, stunned on their mounts, for a space. Clay waited—waited. Then he heard their whooping, their jeering, their laughter, laughter that swelled to Homeric proportions. He watched them begin slapping at each other with their hats and gigging their surprised horses into sunfishing and humpbacking. Once more laughter had returned to ease the tension in the Patchsaddle crew.

Rose Lansing spoke to Clay. "It has worked, but I still pity you when they catch you."

"There's a creek with real water in it about two miles farther on," Clay said. "That is, if my map is correct. We'll hit it by sundown. There's a trading post and army fort a couple of miles east if the map is still right. We'll lay the drive over for a day or two so that the boys can really cool off. They can ride into the post in shifts to whoop it up a little."

"What's the name of this place?" Rose Lansing asked suspiciously.

"I believe it's called Comanche Ford," Clay said reluctantly.

"So that's it," she said, her lips pursed. "I'm quite sure you have heard of it. And so has everybody else. It's worse than this Hackberry. It's so wicked no decent person is safe there. Outlaws, cutthroats, gamblers and—and—"

"And painted women," her daughter said.

Young Lonnie Randall had been listening. "Man, oh, man!" he breathed. "Comanche Ford! I can hardly wait till I git there. I'll shore give that place a spin."

"Well, you're one young one who'll never see it if I can prevent it," Rose Lansing said. "I could never face your poor mother when we get home if I let you go into that den of iniquity."

Lonnie dashed his hat on the ground. "I never did have no luck!" he raged.

Clay waited until the crew had calmed and dressed. He cautiously returned to the herd. They had resumed their places as before. They were suspiciously silent, making no mention of the big event of the day. He kept close watch on them, trying to have eyes in the back of his head.

Sundown came and the brushline of a creek loomed ahead as the drive snailed its way over a long swell in the land—their real destination for the night. The vengeance Clay had been fearing did not come until after the cattle had watered and settled down on the bedground.

Then it struck. Jem Rance engaged his attention at the

wagons, with an inquiry about some detail in connection with the first night trick with the herd. The loop of a lariat descended over his shoulders and tightened. He leaped aside—and stepped into another loop which heeled him as a calf would be heeled on its way to the branding fire. The cousins Cass and Des were handling the ropes.

The crew surrounded him, whooping and grinning. They had cut a bony, high-backed steer from the herd and had left it tied up in the brush nearby. Clay was carried there and placed astride the steer—facing the wrong way.

"Ride 'em, cowboy!" they whooped, and sent the steer lumbering and pitching into the stream with Clay aboard, fully clothed.

They stood howling and jeering as he was thrown by the outraged steer. They were happy. They mudded him when he came to the surface and tried to scramble his way to dry land. They finally permitted him to come ashore. He floundered to a sandbar and sat down, gasping. He pried off his boots, poured water from them. They joined him, joshing him, telling him that they'd skin him alive if he ever pulled a "batter," their term for a joke, on them again.

At the wagons Rose Lansing and Rachel had a special meal ready, topped off with hot dried apple pie, generously sprinkled with brown sugar and nutmeg.

Clay changed to dry garments and sat in the background, content. The antagonisms, the petty irritations, the endless discomforts and hardships—and the danger—were forgotten. At least for the moment. Men who had been at the point of blows hours before were now swapping tall stories and telling it big and long. Once more they were a crew, working together.

The men turned in, one by one. Rose Lansing and Rachel and Cindy retired. Only Ann remained. The cookfire embers cast warm, flickering shards of light. On the distant bedground they could hear Parson Jones and Micah singing softly, reassuringly to the cattle in their deep, melodious voices.

Ann sat with arms folded around her knees, staring dreamingly into the fire. She finally spoke. "It's over."

Clay stirred from his own reverie. "You mean the crew? For a while, anyway. But they're only human. We've got a long, tough way to go. They'll likely get stretched out again. That's why I want to give them a blowout in Comanche Ford. The trail gets to a man, and he's got to get away from it for a spell. A man needs to cut loose or explode. I'll have to think of something else when things get edgy again."

"I wasn't thinking of the crew," she said. "I was thinking of us."

He looked at her, and she nodded. "The Lansings and the Burnets," she said. "It's over. The feud. That's what I meant."

Clay did not speak. Her voice was low, level as she resumed. "I was a fool. Stubborn, spoiled. I was the one who tried to keep it alive—the hatred of the Burnets. I had been taught from childhood to believe you were evil. I know now how wrong I was."

"How wrong we all were," Clay said.

She arose, moved nearer, and sat close beside him. "I had to say these things," she said. "I *had* to know how you feel. You see, my punishment for my conceit in the past is that I'm now falling in love with you."

Clay looked at her, feeling the blood drain from his face. He was thinking of Hatcher's Run. "You must never say a thing like that again!" he said hoarsely.

She sat for a space, all her surrender in her eyes—and all the hurt. "There's something else, isn't there?" she finally said, her lips quivering. "There's something between us. It's something about my brother. About Phil."

He wanted to take her in his arms and tell her how

wonderful she was, how much he desired her, tell her that she was the tranquillity he had always sought.

"I'm sorry," he said.

She continued to sit like a statue for a time. "There's torment in you," she said. "I want to help you, but you won't let me. It was the war. Something in the war. I can't fight ghosts."

She arose and left him, entering the tent. Clay continued to sit there. The entire camp was silent. He was still sitting there long after the embers of the fire had faded into gray ashes. Parson Jones and Micah continued to sing their sad songs in the night.

Presently the Parson rode in, awakened Ace and Zeno to stand the midnight watch, turning over to them the heavy silver watch that belonged to Ham Marsh and which was the official timepiece for the crew. They pulled on pants, shirts, and boots, buckled on guns and spurs, and rode away to the herd, still yawning and heavy-eyed. The Parson and Micah, their cocktail shift ended, turned in. They knew Clay was sitting awake in the background alone with his thoughts, but they did not intrude.

However, after a time, the Parson spoke from his bed. "Do you want to talk, my son?"

"Does it show on me that plain?" Clay asked.

"Not for all eyes, perhaps, but I've been privileged to carry on the Lord's work, so that it is possible I see farther than the others. You carry a great burden, Clay. Greater than the responsibility of these cattle and all us humans. You desire a woman, but you cannot claim her. Would it help if you told me why?"

"A man can't talk himself out of the deepest pit of hell, Parson," Clay said. "I had to send twelve men to their deaths. One was an enemy of mine. I could have gone myself, but I had an obligation to two hundred other men. That's the whole of it."

"I see," the Parson said wearily. He lay silent for a long

time, but evidently could find no more words to say. Finally he wrapped the blanket around him again, and Clay was left alone once more.

When morning came, Clay picked by lottery the half of the crew that would be first to visit Comanche Ford. He talked Rose Lansing into advancing each man ten dollars from the reserve fund. Over the objections of the men, he insisted that they leave their guns at the wagons. "I can't afford to lose any more riders on this trip, now that you've learned to be drovers," he said. "No guns."

The group returned at midnight, singing, staggering, and hilarious. And broke. Cass sported a fancy red garter as a sleeve supporter. Ham Marsh flaunted a lacy feminine pair of pantaloons, which he hastily concealed when Rose Lansing appeared from the tent. Expecting the worst, she had remained awake. She was swathed in a heavy dressing gown, and felt that she had been vindicated in her fears. "Look at them!" she said to Clay. "They call themselves men. Why, they're worse than children. Even Ezra Jones is drunk. And he's a *preacher!*"

"Right now he's a trail driver," Clay said. "And a good one."

"He's a disgrace to his preachings," she said. "I'm going to give him a piece of my mind when he sobers up."

Clay, helped by the sober men in camp, headed the celebrants to their blankets. Clay counted noses. "Where's Nate Fuller?" he asked.

"Nate got rambunctious, an' tried to run Comanche Ford up a tree," Q explained. "He got throwed in the calaboose. The marshal allowed that five dollars fine an' three dollars costs was needed, but by that time none of us had more'n a total of two simoleans among us."

"Imagine!" Rose Lansing said acidly. "Nate Fuller, of all people. A married man, with children. How will I ever be able to face Aimee Fuller when I get home—if I ever dare go home after all this?"

"I'll bail him out when I ride in tomorrow with the other half of the crew," Clay said. "The boys will need the same financing these drunks had, and I'll need a little extra to get Nate out of the *cárcel*."

"You mean we've got to go through all this again!" she moaned. She threw up her hands in defeat and fled to her tent.

Q, who was not so noisy as his companions, spoke to Clay alone. "I run into a feller in Comanche Ford who knows you," he said. "Leastways, when he found out that this outfit hails from down San Dimas way, he asked if any of us happened to know a man named Clay Burnet."

"Who was he?"

"I don't recall him mentionin' his name," Q said. "But he seemed mighty interested when he found out that Clay Burnet was boss of this drive. I got the impression that he might have soldiered with you." He paused, then added, "I also got the feelin' that he wasn't exactly a buddy o' yours. He looked like he'd seen more of the war than he needed. Gaunt, thin, like a steer that had wintered mighty poor. Eyes burnin' out from deep in the sockets. Gave me the creeps, like I was seein' a ghost."

Clay felt a cold, bristling sensation at the back of his neck. "What did he look like?" he asked.

"He wasn't big," Q said. "I'd say about five, eight. Hair had been black, but was sort of a mouse gray now, though he couldn't be any older'n you. Does that mean anything?"

"No." The clammy sensation faded a trifle. Phil Lansing had been tall, fair-haired. At any rate Phil Lansing must be in his grave back there at Hatcher's Run. "I knew a lot of soldiers," he added. "Maybe I'll run into him tomorrow."

"You still going in with the boys?"

Clay knew he was being warned. "Why not?"

"Be sure and pack a gun," Q said. "I already told you I don't think this jigger is friendly."

The next morning Clay hid his gun and holstered belt in

his saddle jacket, which he rolled and laced on the horse as he prepared to ride with the second group to Comanche Ford. He continued to ban weapon carrying on the part of his companions. "I don't want anybody brought back on a plank, or heading for Texas with a posse after him," he told them. He did not mention that he was breaking his own rule because of Q's warning.

The settlement was a step or two down from even the crudeness of Hackberry. It straggled among thin timber along a small stream, whose banks had been flattened by the freight and Army wagons which used the military trail through this area. Its nucleus was an Army fort, built of logs, and a stage station of rock. Both had walls thick enough to stand off arrows and bullets. Passing by the fort, whose gates were open, Clay noted that the garrison was thin. The sentry on duty informed him that the major part of the command was in the field hunting raiding Indians. A gaggle of some score of shabby buildings fronted on the crooked street.

"It'll look purtier after we've cut the dust from our gullets with a slug or two of refreshments," Beaverslide said.

"Nothin' will improve the looks of such females as I've seen," Zeno said glumly, peering at the harrigans who beckoned from doors and windows.

Clay visited the jail, paid the fine and costs that freed Nate Fuller, got his horse out of the livery, and sent him on his way back to the wagon camp.

He took young Lonnie Randall in tow. Lonnie had prevailed on Rose Lansing to permit the visit. He allowed Lonnie a small glass of beer, which went to Lonnie's head, causing him to stride grandly through the town, viewing the dubious sights, and even ogling a woman or two. Lonnie finally noted that Clay had his holstered six-shooter on his side.

"How come you sweet-talked us cowboys into leavin' our

artillery at the wagons?" Lonnie demanded. "Come to think of it, you ain't drinkin'. Not even a beer."

"That's a lot of thinking," Clay said. "How about some grub, then a little game of pool? There's a parlor down the street."

"Pool?" Lonnie said disgustedly. "Grub? Man, I'm a shaggy wolf from the fork o' the crick, never been curried below the knees. I aim to stand on my laigs an' howl. I don't want no grub. I don't want to waste my time playin' pool. I got other notions."

Clay steered him, almost forcibly, into a beanery that promised to be a speck cleaner than its competitors. They ate the usual buffalo steak and fried spuds, canned tomatoes and coffee that Lonnie allowed was heavy enough to float a railroad spike.

Afterward, they made their way to the billiard parlor. Lonnie, resigned to his fate as Clay's companion, broke the wedge of balls on a pool table with a vicious drive of the cue. "Wait'll we git to this Missouri town," he said. "Then I'll cut loose an' take the whole danged place apart."

"Missouri is a state, not a town," Clay said. He drove a ball into a pocket. He paused, watching two of the Patchsaddle crew pass by on the sidewalk. Zeno and Bass. They were walking high in their boots, eyes alight and eager for action.

Clay sighed. "Chances are I'll have some more of 'em to bail out of jail by dark," he predicted.

A red-nosed, unkempt man owned the place. Clay and Lonnie were the only patrons at this afternoon hour. Now a newcomer entered. He was only a silhouette against the sun as he moved through the door. Clay was standing, cue grounded, watching Lonnie prepare to attempt a bank shot.

"Hello, Captain." Clay turned, peering.

The arrival laughed harshly. "No, I'm not a ghost, cap. But I've come back to haunt you."

"Owens," Clay said slowly. "Joe Owens."

"Correct, cap. Corporal Joseph P. Owens, listed as missing in action at Hatcher's Run, near Petersburg, Virginia, an' presumed dead. You recollect the place, I reckon."

"I remember," Clay said.

"You ought to. You sent twelve of us out to take on an army of Yankees so you could save your own skin and—"

"So I could save two hundred other men, along with six pieces of artillery, and pull back to close a break in General Lee's line, which we did," Clay said.

Joe Owens moved away from the flare of the doorway. He was no longer a black shadow. He had been a young, happy-go-lucky soldier, moon-faced, lighthearted. He was now skin and bones, his hair colorless, his thin wrists dangling from the sleeves of a ragged shirt that was too small. As Q had said, his eyes burned out from deep in their sockets. He wore the weight of premature age.

"Unlucky for you, cap," Owens said, "only ten of us died over that ridge. I thought I was the only one still alive till I run into Phil Lansing a couple of weeks ago right here in Comanche Ford. Sergeant Phil Lansing. I reckon you remember him also, don't you, cap?"

"I remember him," Clay said levelly.

"I sorta washed ashore here in this place a few months ago, takin' jobs skinnin' for buffalo hunters, swampin' out saloons, doin' any odd jobs that nobody else would do," Owens went on. "I was hit by a Minié ball, an' was picked up still alive by the bluebellies. I wound up in a Yank prison hospital an' camp until the war ended. Sergeant Lansing, it turned out, had been hit too, but came through alive. They kept him a lot longer, for he was hurt real bad, an' then he wouldn't agree to sign parole, for he thought the Yanks was foolin' him about the war bein' over. So they jest kept him in a Yank prison until he saw the light. Do you know what it was like to be a prisoner of war?"

"I'd like to help you, Corporal," Clay said.

"Help me? Do you think I want help from a man who

was responsible for what I went through? I ought to put a bullet in you as you stand there."

The pudgy proprietor came to life in the barrel chair in which he was sitting. He produced a pistol and its maw was directed at Joe Owens. "I don't want no killin' in my place, fella," he said. "If'n you got to settle this, take it outside."

"Keep your hair on," Owens said. "I ain't goin' to rub out this yella-belly. I'd consider it a pleasure, but I want him to sweat a little while he waits for it to happen. And I promised Phil Lansing I wouldn't rob him of the fun."

He leered at Clay. "Sergeant Lansing said that all that keeps him alive is that he wants to put a slug in your guts. He was on his way back to the San Dimas country when I run into him here at the Ford. He aimed to look you up when he got there. He must have missed your outfit somewhere down the trail, but he's had time to git home by this time an' learn that you're headin' north. My hunch is that he's well on his way back to find you."

Owens let that sink in for a space. "It could be that the sarge is close around already, cap. From now on, every hour, every minute, you can expect another ghost to show up from the battlefield in Virginia. His name will be Phil Lansing, and he has a bullet in his gun with your name on it. He aims to put you in your grave like you tried to put him in his. He knows he's supposed to be dead, an' he let it ride that way. He didn't want you to be warned, so you could light out. He wanted it to be a surprise. Maybe I made a mistake in tellin' you this. Maybe you'll run for it, but I just couldn't deny myself the satisfaction of seein' your face when I told you that, from now on, you can think of every minute as likely to be your last."

Owens walked out of the place, his thin figure blotting out the glare of the sun for an instant. His scuffing footsteps faded on the sunbaked clay sidewalk.

Lonnie Randall had stood pop-eyed, mouth gaping, still

poised for the bank shot, frozen in that position. He looked at Clay and finally managed to speak. "Good gosh! What are you goin' to do, Clay?"

"It's your shot," Clay said. "Side pocket, you say. I say a quarter to your nickel that you miss."

Lonnie missed. By a wide margin. Clay moved to the table. His was also a bank shot. A difficult try. He stroked the cue ball evenly. It clicked against the target ball which rebounded from a cushion, crossed the table, and dropped into a pocket.

Lonnie glanced nervously toward the door. "I reckon I don't want to play any longer," he said.

Clay racked his cue and paid the proprietor, who had put away his pistol. "Did you hear anything said in here?" he asked the man.

"Not me," the owner said hastily. "I've learned to live all these years by stayin' out of other folks' affairs."

"I'll be coming back this way after we deliver the herd," Clay said. "If I was in the mood I could build a fire under you as long as a Mex lariat."

He and Lonnie walked out of the place. "Holy gee whiz!" Lonnie breathed. "Phil Lansing's still alive. Wait 'til I tell Missus Rose an' Miss Ann that their—"

He broke off, peering at Clay. He gazed for seconds. In that brief space he matured considerably, grew grave, and bore a burden. "Maybe I better not," he finally said. "Maybe I better forget I ever saw Joe Owens."

Clay's silence was his answer. They walked along the hot sidewalk, past the doors of saloons and music houses. "What are you going to do, Clay?" Lonnie finally asked.

"Drive the herd on through to Missouri."

"But—but—"

"Nothing's changed. Why should it be?"

"But—but what about Miss Ann? She likes you a lot. I've seen the way she looks at you."

"You must be imagining things, Lonnie."

"If her brother killed you, or you had to kill him, why it would just break her heart. It would—"

The enormity of it was too much for Lonnie. He went silent, staring into an adult world that he had never imagined—a tangled world made up of terrifying conflicts.

CHAPTER 10

Clay and Lonnie herded the happy members of the crew back to the wagons at midnight and wrangled them to bed. The great spree was over.

"Thank the merciful Heaven that none of them were killed," Rose Lansing said. She and Ann and Rachel had remained awake, with hot, black coffee ready. "I hope we don't have to go through anything like this again." She glared accusingly at Clay.

"Not unless they get ranicky again," Clay said. "Maybe we can make it to Missouri before that happens. Then my guess is that we'll see some real fireworks."

"May the good Lord spare me from seeing it," she said.

Clay mounted and rode to the bedground to visit the men on the middle shift to see how the herd was faring. A half moon swam in a clear sky. The only sounds that came from the cattle on this peaceful night were contented sounds.

No sound, except the hard, heavy slam of a rifleshot. Before the report could reach Clay's ears he heard the crackling of displaced air. A bullet had passed within inches of him.

It struck his horse in the back of the head. The animal was killed in its tracks. It pitched forward in a somersault. Clay wore only a right spur, and it caught in the stirrup. He could only try to throw himself aside and hope the horse would not fall on him, or that he would not sustain a broken leg.

His foot came free in time and he managed to roll clear of the animal's weight as it lurched in its death throes. He got shakily to his knees. The breath had been driven from him. He crouched there, wheezing heavily, trying to get at his six-shooter. His holster had been twisted around by his fall. Still half stunned, he had the sensation of moving sluggishly in a nightmare. He expected another bullet. He believed the shot had come from the shadows a considerable distance to his right.

He heard the faint pound of hoofs receding. At the same moment the herd took off in a stampede, the animals alarmed by the shot.

He realized he was right in the path of the stampede—on foot. He remembered Tom Gary in that instant. He started to run, trying to estimate the direction of the stampede and to hope that he was taking the shortest way out of its path. But that could only be guesswork.

A rider loomed up, screaming his name. The arrival was Ann Lansing. Her hair was a dark, rippling cascade in the moonlight, and she was bare-armed, wearing only a skirt and a camisole, evidently having been in the act of turning in for the night. She had appropriated one of the night horses that were always kept at the wagons, saddled, for use of the men who would go on the late bedground tricks.

"Here!" Clay shouted.

She came riding toward him, leaning and offering an arm, which he seized and swung up behind her. She veered the horse and rode clear of the oncoming stampede.

"What happened?" she shouted above the uproar. "I heard a shot. What happened to your horse?"

"Killed," Clay said. "It was rustlers, I reckon, stampeding us so that they could get away with some beef."

It was an answer that didn't answer anything. Stampeding trail drives so that theft of scattered cattle would be easier, was a common practice. But that did not explain the single shot and the fact that this shot had killed Clay's horse. She seemed to sense that she would get no further answer, and did not pursue the matter.

There was nothing more that Clay could tell her. How could he say that he believed it had been her brother who had tried to murder him?

She took him to the wagons where he roped out a new horse from the *remuda* and rigged it with a worn saddle that was carried as a spare. He took off in pursuit of the crew that had cleared out of camp to ride down the stampede.

As a stampede it didn't amount to much. The cattle were paunchful of water and grass, and in no mood to run far. The crew already had them milling. The riders who had just returned from Comanche Ford were nursing aching heads and vowing that if they ever touched another drop of red-eye they hoped someone would take a blacksnake whip to them.

They had all heard the rifleshot and knew that Clay's horse had been killed. They had questions on their tongues, questions that only he and Lonnie Randall could answer. But the questions were not asked. It was taken for granted that if Clay had anything to say he would say it.

They found Clay's dead horse. What damage had been done to the rigging could be repaired. When daybreak came, men of the crew scouted the country. But the stampede had gone over the brushy area from which the shots had been fired. Sifting any particular trail from the maze of hoof and horse tracks was impossible, particularly with only moonlight to help.

"Get what sleep you can," Clay told the crew. "We're throwing them on the trail at daybreak. We've lost enough time here."

He saw worry darkening Ann Lansing's eyes. She knew something was wrong—something that concerned the visit to Comanche Ford. But she asked no questions.

Clay did not turn in, remaining with the three men he had named off to stay with the herd. None of them mentioned the shot that had been fired. The fact they kept so carefully away from that subject showed that they did not believe that rustlers had been responsible. They knew that shot had been aimed at someone. Aimed to kill. And Clay had been the target.

The night faded. Rachel clanged the triangle at the wagon as a signal that sleep was ended and that a new day was starting for the Patchsaddle crew. The swift breakfast was served, the herd thrown on the trail. The cattle were tractable in spite of the night's stampede. They reeled off nearly twenty miles before dusk.

Clay followed the foreman's routine, riding two miles to one for the members of the crew, answering questions, making decisions as to route and procedure. The herd was a machine, half a mile long, mindless and stolid, but packed always with explosive energy that might erupt from the slightest cause.

A stampede from a neighboring herd that was paralleling their route three miles to the east came thundering across the prairie in late afternoon, with riders spurring desperately to swing the leaders north. Clay and his men braced, expecting their Patchsaddle cattle to join in the run. But the Patchsaddles moved placidly along, letting the running cattle race past only a few hundred yards ahead of Blanco and other leaders. Clay sent some of the men to help the harassed crew of the spoiled drive. They came back at dark, tired and vowing they'd never seen such blundering handling of cattle.

Two days later they forded the Canadian River, which was high and swift. The herd, veterans of the trail now, arched across the current in a column beautiful to behold and especially beautiful to a herd boss. Clay had led the way. He sat on his dripping horse on the far bank, watching the long string of cattle snake across the stream. Blanco came ashore, followed by his pals, the calico steer, the big twist-horn cow, the playful black one known as Clown, and Moose, so named because of the width of his horns.

The animals in the herd were becoming individuals. Even more so were the men. There was Beaverslide, for instance. Clay had tabbed the old-timer at the start as a complainer and a troublemaker. On the contrary, Beaverslide had never mentioned hardship, never objected to drag duty or to standing double-guard on stormy nights when the herd was on the roam.

And there were Parson Ezra Jones and Nate Fuller. They had no future when they had started the drive, but now they were proud men in their patches and colorless, washed-out denims, linseys, and butternuts. They had brought a herd up through hundreds of miles of Texas into the perilous Nations. They had seen country they had never expected to see. Now they wanted to see more.

One by one, group by group, they came stringing ashore, the cattle, the men. The wagon was rafted across on floats of dead cottonwood trunks that Q and the men roped from sandbars and lashed together. Rachel and Rose Lansing rode the wagons, watching over their precious mules which swam strongly.

Rachel, especially, was now an experienced wagoneer, who feared no stream, no distance. Clay remembered a day now more than a week in the past when the mules, which hated snakes above all other dangers, had taken off in a runaway when they found themselves amid a colony of hissing, buzzing rattlers. The wagon had capsized in the midst of this horror, but Rachel had freed the tugs, releasing the mules, then had climbed higher on the frame of the vehicle, with Cindy in her arms until help arrived.

"Shucks, I ain' skeered o' snakes," she had told Bass. "I been livin' wid 'em all my life. Have you ever seen a real Texas rattler, Mister Bass? Dey grow ten feet long down whar I come from. Dey use 'em fer bullwhips down thar. Sorry I spilled de wagon, but it don't look like it's gumbled up too bad."

The oldsters like the Parson and Beaverslide clung together in camp, for they found that their yarnings of a past
that was fresh to them and ancient to the younger ones,
drew only polite, forced interest outside their own age circle.
And Q, with his alphabet friends, formed their own group.
There were the three women and Cindy. Then there was
Clay, and there was Micah, islands who stood alone. But
when it came to moving the herd they were a unit, pulling
together, bound by a common pride in their accomplish-
ment.

Micah's horse came splashing ashore, and the big black
man unslung his boots which he had tied around his neck.
He cocked an eye at Clay, and said, "You are ridin' kinda
light, ain't you?"

He was referring to Clay's lack of weapons. Since the
attempt on his life, he had not carried even the customary
six-shooter which was looked on as a necessary part of a
trail man's equipment while with the cattle. It was stored
in the supply wagon.

This was the first time the omission had been mentioned,
but Clay knew that everyone in the crew was well aware
of it and was puzzling over it, particularly Micah and Q.
One or the other of these two had been finding a way to
being close to him the greater part of the time since the
shooting and the stampede. Both always carried rifles on
their saddles in addition to their side guns.

"I don't understand you, Claymore," Micah continued.
"Are you *tryin'* to git yoreself bushwhacked? You had no
business ridin' up thar as pilot, after what happened the
other night. You made a good target o' yoreself the way
you pushed ahead o' the cattle jest now."

"That's over with," Clay said. "I've decided it must have
been some Indian who thought he saw a chance to pick off
a *Tejano*."

Q had joined them and was rolling a brown paper cigaret.

"How about that fella that was askin' about you in Comanche Ford?" he observed. "I got the idea he might have had somethin' in his craw ag'in you. Maybe he's the one who notched on you."

"I reckon there are plenty of folks who don't like me," Clay said.

They studied him, baffled. Ann Lansing had ridden up in time to hear what Q had said. She sat silent also, the same worry in her face.

"Anyway, you ought to at least pack a gun," Q said. "I got a feelin' you're goin' to need it. That wasn't any Indian who took that shot at you. Indians don't rack around alone at night—not these days."

Clay broke up that inquiry by riding away. They were forcing him into shaky grounds. It was evident they had quizzed Lonnie Randall, and even though Lonnie hadn't talked, they were aware he was holding something back as to what had taken place in Comanche Ford.

Clay waved his hat. "Keep 'em moving," he shouted. "Don't let 'em overfeed or water, or they'll be no good the rest of the day."

The routine of the drive took over. Men, including Q and Micah, began hazing cattle away from the river. Soon, with Blanco and his pals striding ahead, the Patchsaddle herd was bound northward once more. Now it would be the Arkansas River that lay across their path—the last big hurdle on the way to their Golconda, which was named Missouri.

Clay was glad to escape from searching eyes, especially from the gaze of Ann Lansing. Micah and Q might be right in suspecting that Joe Owens was the one who had fired from the darkness, but always in Clay's mind was a man whom Owens had named as having sworn to kill him. Phil Lansing. That was why he had stored his six-shooter and rifle in the supply wagon. He could not shoot it out with the last of the Lansing line. If he killed Phil Lansing he could never again face Rose Lansing. Above all, he could never face Ann.

He rode pilot again, well ahead of the drive, to the despair of Micah and Q, who rode at the points and could only watch over him from a distance. He nearly paid for his life for disregarding their advice before the day was over.

The sun and the shadows were long-legged hobgoblins that marched stride for stride with a mounted man. A great buffalo herd had gone through this prairie recently, leaving a juggernaut scar of cropped forage, littered with droppings and the wolf-torn carcasses of weaker ones that had been cut from the fringe of the herd.

The sun went down, purple dusk came, and broken ground appeared to the east where a network of gullies and ravines was backed by miles of timberland and brush.

A rifle flashed from one of the coulees. The bullet was a savage thrust that knocked Clay askew in the saddle. The second shot missed. If there was a third, he did not see the flash, for he was letting himself plunge from the saddle to the ground. His horse, a thin-necked, tough sorrel that was the youngest and wildest in his string, took this opportunity to go to pieces and went bucking away, trying to rid itself of the saddle.

He lay flat in tall grass that protected him. He explored his thigh with his hand. He found no blood, no flesh injury. The slug had torn through the folds of the worn bullhide chaps he was wearing, and the only damage was the ragged slit in the leather.

Micah arrived, his horse at full gallop. He had his rifle in his hands. He yanked his mount to a stop, his face a picture of concern. "You hit bad, Claymore?" he asked.

"Not hit at all," Clay said. "It only tore through my leggin's and jerked me around in the saddle."

Micah started to dismount, then thought better of it. He

peered, vengeance in his eyes, and was about to head for the dark gullies, but Clay halted him. "Don't do anything foolish. It might be an ambush. Indians. And whoever did it can be well on his way by this time. It'll be dark soon."

Q and others arrived, Ann Lansing among them. Ignoring Clay's warnings to stay back, the men rode toward the breaks in the prairie. Q was already forming a hangnoose in his lariat.

But in the approaching darkness the network of draws and barrancas defied easy search. All they could report when they returned was that the bushwhacker evidently had investigated the terrain before choosing the spot to shoot from, and had made sure he knew a safe path of escape into the tangled timber beyond.

There was little talk around the wagon fires that night. Clay sat in shadow near the supply wagon, and Micah saw to it that he was shielded by tarps, hung to block points from which a shot might be fired from darkness at a distance.

"Quit babying me," Clay said.

"Now, will you pack a gun, stupid man?" Micah growled.

Clay did not answer. Micah withdrew like a disgruntled crab, complaining in grunts to Q, who shared his disapproval of Clay's obstinacy. And there was another. Clay was again aware that Ann Lansing was studying him moodily. There was an increasing dread in her face.

He tried to avoid her, but she managed to maneuver him apart from the others where they could speak alone. "Do you want to tell me anything?" she asked. "Or would you prefer to tell my mother?"

"I don't know what you mean?" Clay said.

"Whoever keeps trying to kill you will try again," she said. "That's for certain after tonight. Do you still intend to let him do this? Do you still intend to go unarmed, deliberately giving him every chance to murder you?"

Clay did not answer. She waited a moment. When he remained silent, she said, "It's tied in with something that happened back at Comanche Ford, isn't it? Lonnie Randall knows. I can see it in his face. He wishes he didn't know. He's scared, worried. I could probably force it out of him if I tried, but that would not be fair, for he's little more than a boy. I'd prefer that you tell me."

"There's nothing to tell."

"It has something to do with my brother," she said. "Something about Phil. What is it?"

"Stay out of this," Clay said. His voice was hoarse, shaking. "There's nothing for any of us in this but—but—"

He couldn't finish it. She finished it for him. ". . . but death for you—and heartbreak for me. You know how I feel about you. And I'm sure I know how you feel about me."

Clay gazed at her, agonized. "You've got to forget all that, stop saying things like that."

"Phil is alive, isn't he?" she said. "You believe he is the one who is trying to kill you!"

She saw that he could not deny it. She covered her face with her hands. "Oh, God!" she sobbed. "My own brother! He's trying to murder you! Why? The feud? Is it that awful feud?"

She tried to clasp her arms around him. Clay held her away. "No," he said. "That's impossible. We must not."

She believed that the gulf that had always separated the Burnets and the Lansings had opened again. She stood looking into grisly, appalling possibilities.

"You'd let him kill you, rather than try to defend yourself and kill him," she said brokenly. "Because of me, because you love me. I know you do. I know you will never tell me that in words, but it's true. Don't you understand that if you are dead I'll have this to live with all my life? I won't let this awful thing happen. I'll find Phil. I'll stop him, make him see how wrong he is."

Her mother came through the darkness and took her

daughter in her arms. "What is it, darling?" she asked gently. "What has happened?"

Ann could not answer. She could not share her burden with her mother, knowing the grief and terror it would bring. She could only weep in Rose Lansing's arms as they walked away together.

CHAPTER 11

When Clay rode ahead of the herd, piloting the way, as the drive was thrown on the trail in the morning, he found that he had a companion. Ann Lansing was at his side, riding stirrup to stirrup with him.

She did not speak. Her face, with its delicate, high cheekbones, was a thin wedge, framed by the chin strap that held her hat on her plaited hair. Her eyes seemed larger, and there were dark shadows under them, evidence of a sleepless night.

She had been in the habit of carrying a pistol in a saddle holster, but the holster was now empty. So was the rifle sling. Clay was again unarmed.

He looked back. Q was riding right point, with the taciturn big, bronzed man who called himself Zeno at left point in place of Micah who had dropped back to first swing. Zeno packed a six-shooter, but in place of the big, bullhide holster he had used in the past while in the saddle, the gun was now in a tied-down, halfbreed affair—a gunman's equipment.

Clay knew that the weapon had always been within quick reach of the big man, day or night. He had never asked questions of Q as to the past of his companions, but on occasions he had seen Zeno brush up on marksmanship when the firing was too remote from the cattle to cause alarm. He had learned that Zeno was swift on the draw and deadly of aim, and that he continually honed these skills, as though he knew that someday he would need them against someone. There was dark tragedy beneath the casual, easygoing manner of the big man. In his past lurked depths that Clay hoped would never be plumbed.

Micah was riding fully armed, even to a belt knife. These men, Clay understood, were his bodyguards, self-appointed. As for Ann Lansing, she had gone even further. She was stationing herself where she believed her presence would not only serve to deter a bullet from her brother, but where she might even be able to offer her own body as a shield. Knowing the Lansings, he knew she would do such a thing. He also knew that nothing he might say could change her decision.

A lump came in his throat as he considered the devotion of this girl and the three men. He remembered little Cindy saying that strong men could not weep. Micah and Q might feel that they had great obligation to him, but Zeno owed him nothing but the loyalty that had evolved during the days of hardship and monotony on the trail. Clay felt that Zeno, too, must have his ghosts which might rise from the past at any time to put a bullet in his back.

One of those ghosts was near at hand now for Zeno. It was mid-afternoon when Clay rose in the stirrups, squinting ahead. Dust was rising in the distance.

"What can it be?" Ann asked, peering.

Strange objects were taking form, miraged to fantastic proportions by the reflections of the sun. Gaily painted vehicles became visible, with streamers whipping from their gilded turrets. Some were drawn by ponies bearing purple and golden cockades. One had a camel and bullock in harness. Another was drawn by mules, painted with stripes to represent zebras.

"Gypsies!" Q shouted.

"*Comancheros!*" Micah pronounced.

"Mexican circus!" Ann exclaimed.

"Looks to me like a little bit of all three," Clay said.

The exotic caravan evidently had been aware that it would meet the trail drive and had decked itself out for the occasion. It had been bound down the trail for the Indian country, and for Mexico, no doubt. Now that it had sighted the oncoming Texas trail men and their cattle, the wagons swung into a circle, halted, and prepared to camp.

As the distance lessened Clay heard music—cymbals, drums, bells. Women in Oriental and Spanish costumes appeared, cavorting and beckoning. They had bells around their ankles. Men joined them, turning handsprings and some juggling gilded spheres.

"Go fetch my guns," Clay said. "Rifle and sidegun."

Ann, surprised, hesitated. Clay rose in the stirrups and signaled Rose Lansing and Rachel to halt the wagons and camp. He waved his hat, ordering the crew to throw the cattle off the trail.

"Surely you're not afraid of that scabby bunch, are you?" Ann asked. "Look at them now that we can see. Paint peeling from the wagons, those poor animals skin and bones, men who look like cutthroats. And those women! Such hussies, and some of them half naked."

"They're bad enough," Clay said. "They're not exactly harmless, even by themselves. Some look like genuine gypsies, and my guess is some were *Comancheros* in the days when there was money in trading guns to the tribes. It looks like they all flocked together to make whatever living they could off the country. But they've got help. Big help."

He pointed. Another haze of dust was rising in the wake of the gypsy caravan. "Indians!" Ann exclaimed tremulously.

"Fetch the fieldglass as well as the guns," Clay said. He waited until she had made a fast round trip to the wagons, which were being camped by the women drivers, and adjusted the glasses.

"Some are Indians," he said slowly. "But not all."

"What else could they be?" she asked.

"Nothing good. Some call them border runners, or Bully Boys, or Jayhawkers. What they actually are is an outfit of cutthroats who prefer to call themselves unconstructed rebels. Guerrillas, in other words. During the war they joined up with renegade Indians to kill and rob both Secesh and Unionists. And they stayed in business after the war ended. I was warned to look out for them. They're bad business. There's likely a single name for every man in that outfit. Murderer."

"How many are there?"

"I can't tell exactly. I'd say at least thirty, maybe more. That's not counting the ones with the circus. Now circle the herd and tell the men to come into the wagons."

"The cattle?"

"Will have to take their chances," Clay said. "We may be in for a fight, we may not."

She rode away, spurring her horse, fright in her eyes. Clay rode to the wagons. Scanning the terrain he selected a position clear of all but scrub brush, with a scatter of small boulders which would serve as barricades against attackers. A wide, shallow wash, dry except for a tiny trickle of water in its center, broke through the flat a short distance beyond the site he had selected.

He spotted the wagons so that they would serve as barriers for riflemen. Rose Lansing and Rachel handled this task, backing the mule teams expertly into the positions that satisfied him.

The crew came in, sober-eyed and tense. At Clay's order, Rose Lansing dealt out rifles and spare ammunition from the supply wagon.

"It could be Major Blood, along with Stone Buffalo's bunch," Q said. "There was talk at Hackberry that they was ridin' together an' had jumped some wagon trains an' a trail outfit or two. Ever hear of 'em?"

"Who hasn't?" Clay said.

The renegade who was known as Major Blood had made a black reputation as a guerrilla during the war, having been the leader of a band of cutthroats that had preyed on settlers whose men were with the armies. Blood's speciality, in addition to murder and looting, had been the kidnaping of white children whom he sold to the Indians, then profited by acting as go-between in ransoming the captives back to grieving parents. Blood was said to have once been a freebooter on the Caribbean, and Clay had been told that the man glorified in dressing like a pirate and that he used the Jolly Roger as his emblem.

Stone Buffalo was a Commanche chief who had taken his sacred oath to kill all white invaders of the buffalo country and was followed by Indians of half a dozen tribes who joined in that cause.

Clay noticed that Q was intently watching Zeno. "Take it easy, Matt," Q said. "There's still a chance it isn't Blood's outfit."

Zeno, whose real front name evidently was Matt, was standing gazing fixedly toward the oncoming body of guerrillas. He did not turn, as he still sat on his horse peering. The guerrillas halted near where the gypsy circus had pulled up, preparing to camp. The music and tinkle of bells went on, along with the distant, tantalizing laughter of women.

"Fix barricades," Clay said. "For the women. Wagon boxes, boulders, whatever is handy."

He continued to watch Zeno, chilled by something in the man's face. And Q was watching also. "Don't do anything crazy, Matt!" Q spoke urgently.

Zeno finally spoke. "It *is* Blood. I see him now. He's the big man wearin' the red sash an' the flair boots, like a pirate. Like the woman-killer he is. Like the child stealer!"

Zeno stirred his horse. Clay had never seen such cold rage in the face of a human, such consuming desire to kill. Zeno meant to ride into the guerrilla camp alone, but Q seized the bit chains of the horse, halting the animal. "Take it easy, Matt," he said.

"I've waited three years for this," Zeno said. "I've thought of nothing else."

Clay interceded. "Whatever it is, Zeno, we can't let you go alone into that nest of killers, and we can't go with you. We're outnumbered, and we'd be wiped out. The odds are up to five to one against us."

Zeno drew a long breath. Some of the frenzy faded out of him. "Four years ago I enlisted in the Union Army," he said. "I had a wife and a daughter. My daughter was seven years old. I was a farmer on the Missouri border. That man over there hit my farm with his renegades one night. They murdered my wife and her parents and sold my daughter to the Kiowas. A company of border militia raided the Kiowa camp later on and found my daughter— dead. She'd been killed by the squaws when the soldiers hit the camp. All I want is to get this man who calls himself Major Blood in front of me, an' tell him I'm goin' to kill him. Then I'll start shootin'. I'll put bullets in his arms. Then I'll break his legs. Then I'll put a slug in his heart. I've practiced. I've made a gunman of myself, just waitin' this chance."

The Parson moved closer, and was listening. "Do not take the Lord's work in your own hands, my son," he said. "Vengeance is mine, saith the Saviour."

Zeno looked at him without seeing him. The Parson shook his head, knowing that his appeal was useless.

Rose Lansing spoke. "Look!"

Two riders had left the guerrillas and were approaching the wagons. One was a leather-clad, mahogany-skinned man, mounted on a black horse, who bore in his right hand a white pennant fixed to the shaft of a spear. He bore an ingratiating, white-toothed smile. Accompanying him, on a cockaded, spotted pony, was a young woman wearing a male Spanish costume of brocaded vest, pleated shirt and belled, laced velvet breeches over high-heeled boots. She was wickedly comely, but obviously hardened to her way of life. Like her companion, she was of Mexican-Indian blood.

She returned the gaze of Ann and Rose Lansing with mocking challenge.

Clay swung into the saddle and rode to meet them, halting them at a distance, for he was sure one of their purposes was to assess their numbers and the strength of their position. He found Ann had joined him. "Go back," he said.

"No," she said, and he did not press the point.

"*Buenas tardes!*" the man cried. "We greet you, *señor*. You are from Texas, no? And with the cattle to sell in the north. We are very, very happy to meet. We invite you to our camp where you will feast and drink, and be entertained."

"*Gracias,*" Clay said. "I regret to say we are in a hurry to get to market. My men need rest tonight. We regret our inability to accept your invitation."

The girl spoke. "I will tell your fortune, *Tejano*. I will tell you whether you are in for much trouble."

"And does your fortune say that those who cause us trouble may not live long enough to regret it?" Clay asked.

The girl's lips tightened. "Do you not know who is our leader? He will consider your manner an insult."

"We know your leader," Clay said. "He is the woman-killer who calls himself Major Blood."

"Woman-killer?" It was the girl's companion who spoke. His pretense at friendliness had gone. "He will not be happy when he learns what you have called him."

Zeno moved into the foreground. "Then let him come out alone," he said. "I will call him a woman-killer to his face. I am not a woman. Tell him to come out armed. I will let him go for his gun first—before I move. Then I will break his arms with bullets, break his legs, then kill him."

The leathery man peered closer at Zeno. "Who is it who speaks so bravely and who will likely turn tail like a rabbit and run when Major Blood comes to meet this braggart?" he asked Clay.

"His name is Zeno," Clay said. "That's all you need to know."

The pair began to back their mounts away. They were frightened by the cold rage in Zeno. "We won't shoot you in the back," Clay said. "We leave that sort of thing to you people."

The two remained wary until they were at a safer distance. Then they wheeled their mounts and rode at full speed to where the guerrillas had camped a distance apart from the gypsy caravan.

"I can't say you went out of your way to handle that diplomatically," Ann said to Clay. "You might as well have given them a few slaps in the face. Wouldn't it have been better to have?—"

"Acted like we were afraid of them? That's why they sent those *mestizos* here—to find out if we were loaded for bear. They were supposed to size us up, find out how tough we might be."

"But they invited us to—"

"To walk into their spiderweb and be murdered," Clay said. "That gypsy circus is only a trap to bait people like us into easy reach of Blood and Stone Buffalo and their cutthroats. That would be the easiest way for them to get our cattle."

"They're after the cattle?"

"What else? They must know that trail outfits aren't loaded down with cash, especially this one."

"How—how are they going to try to take the herd from us?" she asked, frightened.

"Depends," Clay said.

"On what?"

"On Zeno, and this Major Blood. If Zeno is too fast for Blood, that might settle it, and Blood's outfit might go away. If it goes the other way, we're likely in for it."

She was staring at him with growing horror. "You don't mean you're going to let Zeno fight that terrible man?"

When Clay did not answer she turned to look wildly at the others who were listening. The men of the Patchsaddle crew stood in brooding silence. Zeno, who stood apart, was staring off into the distance. Rachel had Cindy at her side, an arm around the child. Cindy was weeping softly. Even she understood.

Rose Lansing moved to Zeno, took his face between her hands and kissed him on the lips. "I will pray for you, my friend," she said. "We will all pray for you."

Ann whirled on Clay. "No!" she cried. "No! You can't let this go on! Why, this man, this Major Blood, is said to have murdered twenty men in gunfights. Zeno wouldn't have a chance. You've got to put a stop to—"

Her voice faded off. Born and raised on the frontier, she knew the code. Major Blood had been challenged to come out and duel an opponent with his followers looking on. The guerrilla leader had his choice. He could meet the issue or back down. Refusal to meet the challenge would mean loss of face with his men, and perhaps worse. It was the law of the pack that he headed that its leader be all-powerful, or be pulled down.

Her mother came and tried to draw Ann away. She moved free and grasped Clay by the arm. "Don't let Zeno go through with this," she pleaded. "He—he might die. Let him stay here with us. You must stop it. It's your responsibility."

Clay stood, remembering another day when something like this was his burden. A day when powder smoke lay like a curse over the battlefield, pierced by the sheet lightning of cannon fire.

He looked at Zeno. The big man was inspecting his six-shooter, making sure of its action and the charges. It was a long-barreled, single-action Colt, the kind Union officers had carried during the later stages of the war, replacing the heavier cap-and-ball weapons. There was now only a stony purpose in Zeno, a purpose that was not to be thwarted.

Clay moved to him and extended a hand. Neither man spoke. Q and others also shook hands with Zeno. Then Zeno swung into the saddle and rode into the open. He halted his horse when he was midway to the guerrilla camp and sat there in the saddle, motionless, waiting.

There was turmoil in the guerrilla camp. Clay could hear the far, faint sound of excited voices. Faces kept turning in the direction of the Patchsaddle camp. This suddenly quieted.

A rider emerged from among the tawdry wagons of the caravan. He was a broad, paunchy man on a powerful sorrel horse. He wore the jackboots, doublet, and pantaloons of a pirate. A great black beard masked his jowls. He wore a tricornered hat that bore the skull and crossbones in white. He now threw this back to his followers, and came riding forward, bareheaded. His hair was black, thick, and curly. A six-shooter was thrust in his red sash, along with a dagger. A curved sword was in a scabbard at his knee. This was Major Blood.

He was confident, arrogant. He shouted something, an insult, Clay imagined, in Zeno's direction, but the words were lost in the distance. Blood came advancing slowly on the horse, and finally halted some hundred feet from where Zeno waited. The guerrilla leader dismounted. He beckoned Zeno to approach, daring him, taunting him. Major Blood was playing out his role. He knew he must bluster and swagger, knew he must win.

Zeno swung from the saddle, slapped his horse so that it moved out of the way of possible bullets. He stood facing Major Blood. Clay heard Ann and Rose Lansing and Rachel begin to pray. That was the only sound in the Texas camp.

Blood, the killer, was the picture of death itself in the garb he affected, which was so out of place here so far from salt water. Zeno, in dog-eared boots and shirt and breeches that had faded to neutral hue, seemed pallid and inadequate in contrast to the colorful bandit. But Clay's gaze was riveted on the one feature of Zeno's appearance that counted —the holstered six-shooter on his right thigh.

Zeno moved toward Major Blood. They were now within easy shooting range. It came then like gunfights always do—like the wicked flicker of lightning and the crash of thunder. Major Blood's nerve was the first to break. He shouted something and drew. He was very fast. Split-second work. His gun erupted flame, but the trigger was pulled by the finger of a man already doomed.

Zeno had fired first. Clay watched Blood whirl around, his weapon falling from his fingers to the ground. He stood stricken, broken not so much by the impact of the slug, but by the knowledge that he was a dead man.

Zeno fired again, then again. Blood's arms were broken by the slugs. Zeno was keeping his promise that the man would pay. Blood reeled as though in an attempt to run. Zeno fired again, and Blood went down, rolling like a stricken chicken, a leg shattered by the slug.

Zeno moved toward his man. In the silence that followed the gun thunder his voice was distinct. "Remember that little girl you stole the day you scum murdered my wife and parents on a farm near Joplin?"

He raised the gun to fire again. But Ann had left Clay's side and was running toward him. "No!" she screamed. "No! He's dying. Don't do anything more that might be on your conscience the rest of your life. No, Zeno."

Zeno did not fire the shot. Ann reached his side and stood with him. He remained for seconds looking at Blood, who lay writhing in the grass. Ann took the six-shooter from his grasp and swung him around. Then he came walking with her back to the wagons.

Blood's people came scurrying and carried their fallen leader back to the camp. Clay looked at Zeno. Ann still stood, an arm around the dark-haired man. The black, taciturn shadow that had marked Zeno's nature seemed to have lifted. He had not put the finishing shot in the man he had sworn to kill, and Clay felt that Zeno was finding solace in that forbearance now.

Rose Lansing spoke to Clay. "It's over. Thank God. We can throw the herd on the trail and be miles away from this awful place before dark."

"I'm afraid it isn't over," Clay said.

The tawdry gypsy circus was moving onward, stringing in a ragged line over the rolling prairie. But the circus was merely moving out of range, taking its women with it. The main body of guerrillas remained in position. Now they began to mount and move toward the wagons.

They moved in two segments, the white guerrillas being led by the leathery man who had first acted as emissary and who evidently now had taken over in Blood's place. All were armed, with rifles slung in their arms. The Indian contingent, feathers and paint showing, were being directed by a chief who wore only a breechclout and a single eagle feather and had a large shield of buffalo hide poised.

"Stone Buffalo," Q said. "Look! He wants to palaver. I'll side you."

Stone Buffalo had moved ahead of his warriors. They halted and so did the guerrillas as Stone Buffalo advanced, making the sign that he wanted to talk.

Clay, with Q at his side, rode to meet him. Stone Buffalo peered toward the wagons, and it was evident he also was trying to determine the strength of the Texans. His gaze came back to Clay. Stone Buffalo was scarred by time and battle. He was a "Naini" Comanche, a term for that segment of his people who were "alive" and inflexibly committed to oppose any invader of their hunting grounds. The shield was in his left hand; his right hand gripped the handle of a pistol that was thrust in the belt of his breechclout.

Clay looked at the hand on the gun. "You ask palaver, Stone Buffalo, but you are ready to kill."

The chief spoke English fluently. "You are the ones who

have killed. My friend Blood is dead. And you are on the sacred hunting grounds of the red man. Because of you and people like you the buffalo are growing hard to find. We eat birds and rabbit. That is not good for warriors. Because there are no buffalo, we need *vaca* to fill our bellies."

"There are buffalo around," Clay said. "Many more buffalo than cows. Why do you not try to find them?"

Stone Buffalo pointed toward the herd. "We take *vaca*," he said.

Clay raised two fingers. "Two cows," he said. "I will give you two cows to feed your warriors who can't find the buffalo that are so easy for others to hunt."

Stone Buffalo spat contemptuously on the ground. He raised both hands, with all ten fingers extended. He closed them, opened them twice, three times.

"This number we will take," he said. "If we need, we will take more."

Stone Buffalo was saying that he would take forty head of cattle, and that he would take the entire herd if he so desired. To emphasize his demand he looked back, made a gesture, and both the Indians and the guerrillas moved in closer.

"We have many mouths to feed," he said. "Many guns to shoot. You are not so many."

Clay spread all the fingers of one hand. "Five cows," he said. "That is all. We are not so many as your people, but we have guns that shoot all day, and men who never miss. You saw what happened to your Major Blood. It will happen to very, very many of your warriors, and even to you, Stone Buffalo. Five cattle."

Stone Buffalo's dark eyes flickered a little. Clay felt that there was little doubt in the chief's mind that any attempt to rush their position would be costly. He also believed the chief was not in a mood for a fight. A young, tall, wild-eyed warrior left the ranks of the Indians and came riding up to join the chief and began angrily berating him, urging him to fight. But Stone Buffalo continued to waver, evidently deciding to bargain for more cattle. He began lifting his spread fingers again, evidently to reduce his demand, but he never finished the haggling.

A bullet twitched at Clay's hatbrim. It had been meant for him. It missed and struck the young warrior alongside Stone Buffalo, smashing into his shoulder. He would have toppled from the pad saddle, but a moccasined foot caught in the plaited leather sling that served as a stirrup. He managed to hang to his tough-muscled buffalo pony until it stopped rearing.

Stone Buffalo uttered a cry of fury. "You have tried to kill my son!" he screeched. He drew his six-shooter and fired at Clay. But all the horses were rearing, and the shot missed.

Q had drawn and would have shot the Comanche chief, but Clay shouted, "No! Wait! It's a mistake!"

Clay had drawn his own pistol. He could have killed Stone Buffalo, whose pony was still unmanageable, but held his fire. So did Q. The Comanche chief, his face contorted with rage, gained control of his horse, caught the headstall of his son's pony, and rode out of range. The young Comanche was clinging to the neck of his mount.

Clay and Q looked at each other in dismay, then rode back to the wagons, where their people were milling about, guns in their hands.

"We're in fer it now," Q said.

Clay hit the ground in a running dismount. "Who fired that shot?" he demanded.

"Nobody from here," Ann Lansing said. "It came from somewhere beyond the wagons. From the riverbed." Then she cried, "Look!"

Two riders had appeared from the dry wash. One had a rifle in his hands and was covering the man who rode ahead of him.

Rose Lansing uttered a heart-rending cry. "Philip! Philip! My son! My dear son!"

She stood an instant, staring at what she believed was the ghost of her son. She began to sway, and Clay caught her as she fainted.

CHAPTER 12

Ann and Rachel took Rose Lansing's limp body from Clay's arms. Rachel looked at the oncoming riders with terror. "De Lord help us all!" she mumbled. "De graves are givin' up dar daid."

The two women placed Rose Lansing on a blanket near the wagon. Ann arose, leaving the care of her mother to Rachel, and came back to Clay's side.

"Phil!" she called. "Phil, you *are* alive."

Phil Lansing did not answer. He kept his rifle covering the rider ahead of him. He was a thin and emaciated shadow of the dashing, handsome Phil Lansing who had ridden off to war at the age of twenty with the kerchiefs of more than one feminine admirer on his sleeves.

The man Phil Lansing was bringing in was Bill Conners. Even in the weeks since Clay and Conners had fought with fists in Hackberry, the former Loop L foreman had gone farther down the scale. He was grimy, had not shaved in many days, and looked as though he always slept in his clothes. His face beneath its matt of whiskers was bloated; his eyes were hooded and cloudy.

Phil Lansing brought both horses to a stop at a short distance. His sister started to run toward him, but he waved her back. "I'm alive, Ann," he said. "I'm not a ghost. I didn't come back from the grave. I came back from far worse than that."

He looked at Clay. "You know why I'm here, Burnet," he said.

Clay nodded. "Joe Owens told me. I ran into him at Comanche Ford. But I'd like to hear it from your own lips."

"You're hearing it," Phil Lansing said. "I came here to kill you."

"You seem to have lost your touch," Clay said. "You had a reputation as the best sharpshooter in the Texas Brigade. But you've missed me three times."

Lansing slid from his horse. He motioned to Bill Conners to alight also. Conners obeyed listlessly. In him was the fixed despair of a man who had lost the desire to live.

"You ought to know better than that, Burnet," Phil Lansing said. "You should know that when I came after you it would be face to face and not from a bushwhack. It was Conners here who did the missing. At least he missed a few minutes ago and winged that young Comanche. He told me he had a score to settle with you, but that you've been lucky. Your luck has now run out."

"No," Clay said. "I'm happy that you finally showed up. I've been waiting for it. I want it ended."

"I've been on your trail for a long time," Lansing said. "I've been all the way to the San Dimas where I found out that I must have passed you somewhere in Texas. So I headed back north. I came in sight of the herd in time to see that you had got yourselves into a tight fix with that bunch of crossbreeds out there. I took to the arroyo, sighted Conners skulking along. He'd left his horse tied up. I saw him take that potshot, then stopped him as he was trying to get back to his horse to get away. I didn't know what it was all about until he told me. I figured I better bring him in."

"I apologize," Clay said. "Fact is, I never could really bring myself to believe you were notching on my back. But I never thought Conners had the sand to even try that."

"Conners might be satisfied with trying to assassinate you," Phil Lansing said. "But I want you to be looking at me when I throw down on you. I've traveled a long way for that pleasure. Now is the time. You've got a gun on you. Draw!"

Phil Lansing snatched out the six-shooter he was carrying in a holster. He meant to kill. But Clay made no move toward his own weapon.

Ann uttered a scream, and shoved Clay aside, placing herself between him and her brother's vengeance. Phil Lansing could not hold back the shot he intended. The six-shooter roared.

Clay was staggered by her strength, but he steadied himself and clung to her, horrified, believing she had taken the bullet. She continued to grasp him desperately and shield him.

Her brother's shot had missed, partly because he had been shaken by his sister's intervention and partly because she had managed to veer herself and Clay out of line.

Phil Lansing swung the pistol around again, seeking a clear shot at Clay. "No, no!" his sister screamed. "No, Phil! You can't! It's a mistake. It must be a mistake. I am in love with Clay Burnet."

Rose Lansing had revived. She came hurrying shakily into the line of fire and threw her arms around her son. "It *is* you!" she moaned. "My son! My darling son! You *are* alive!"

He tried to wrest free, the fury for vengeance still upon him, but his mother clung. She pushed his pistol down. "Why are you trying to kill Clay Burnet?" she sobbed. "Have you lost your mind?"

"I *am* going to kill him," her son gritted.

With galvanized strength his mother wrested the gun from his hands. "I won't let you do this terrible thing!" she panted. "Oh, my son! My son! You look like a ghost. Where have you been all this time? You were listed as dead. But I never really gave up. Somehow I knew it wasn't so."

"I was wounded in a fight near the end of the war," Phil Lansing said. "I was picked up for dead by Yankee soldiers, but they found that I was alive. I had been hit in a dozen places. I've got a leg that will never be worth much."

For the first time Clay realized that Phil Lansing was favoring a crippled leg.

"I didn't know who I was for months," Lansing continued. "I was in a Yank hospital for weeks. After I was able to move around on crutches I was taken to a penitentiary at Columbus, Ohio, where they were still holding Confederate prisoners that were classified as too dangerous to turn loose. It seems that I was one of the worst of the lot. I didn't remember it, but I had tried to kill some of the hospital people, and had tried to escape several times."

"Why didn't you let us know, my darling son?"

"I had my reasons. It was only a couple of months ago that I really came out of the fog. That was the first time I clearly knew who I was and remembered what had happened."

He looked at Clay. "I remembered it all, Burnet. I remembered everything that happened at Hatcher's Run. I realized that I had been given up for dead by that time. I let it ride that way. The Yankees were glad to get rid of a person like me. I signed the parole and was turned loose. I made it to Kansas by stealing rides on trains and wagons. I got a job swamping for a bull team that was freighting into Texas. That was the direction I wanted to go. I was on my way back to the San Dimas when I ran into another ghost at Comanche Ford a few weeks ago. Joe Owens. He had been a corporal in our outfit. He was the only other one who came out of it alive that day. So you talked to him at the Ford, Burnet?"

Clay nodded. "He told me you were alive and that you'd likely be coming back up the trail to kill me. I've been expecting you."

"I don't understand," his mother said frantically.

"Burnet ordered me and eleven more men to their deaths so that he could save his own skin," her son said icily.

Ann spoke. She was still standing in front of Clay, thwarting his efforts to force her to stand aside. "This is no time for bringing up the old feud, Phil. That's ended. Because of Conners we're now all in deep trouble."

"Is all this true?" Rose Lansing asked hollowly of Clay. "About ordering my son to his death?"

"I gave the order," Clay said.

"But—but—" She couldn't finish it.

Clay looked at Bill Conners. "I didn't give you credit enough, Bill. It probably takes a certain type of nerve, I imagine, to hate a man enough to trail him for weeks and try three times to kill him. But you didn't have quite enough nerve to hold a steady bead."

He looked at Phil Lansing. "Now what?"

"Nothing's changed," Lansing said. "I'm still here for only one purpose."

Clay nodded. "That's your choice. However, I'm afraid you'll have to wait your turn. There are other people who think they have first claim on my scalp—and on yours. We seem to be in this together."

He pointed. Stone Buffalo's warriors were milling around, brandishing weapons. The chief's sonorous voice could be faintly heard, inciting them. The guerrillas had moved in and were listening.

"It'll be a pony charge by the Indians," Clay said. "With Blood's renegades helping. All you men who were in the war know how to act. All take cover. You women, get back of the barricades under the wagons and stay there. Horses can't overrun wagons. Lonnie, you stay under the wagons too."

"Sorry, sir," Lonnie Randall said. "That's only for the women. I'll stay with my father."

"Of course," Clay said. "Of course. And you'll be needed on the fighting line."

He spoke to Phil Lansing. "You will stay near the women and Cindy. If worst comes to worst you know what to do."

He added curtly, "That's an order."

Everyone knew what the order meant. The women and the child were to be killed by Phil Lansing, rather than let them be taken captive. Years of Army discipline prevailed on Phil Lansing. His right hand automatically started to rise to the brim of his ragged hat. Realizing that he had been about to salute the man he was sworn to kill, he stopped the gesture in time.

"I'd prefer that someone else—" he began hoarsely.

His mother spoke. "No, Phil. You are our loved one. Do as Clay Burnet says."

Lansing turned and limped away with the women to make sure they were made as safe as possible. Around Clay the men were grimly preparing to stand attack. Selecting cover, they were looking to their weapons. Clay moved among them, placing them so that their positions protected each other from flanking attack. Clay turned the horses loose and sent them trotting away to freedom to avoid danger from stampeding hoofs.

He sent Bass and Ace worming their way to positions to right and left well beyond their main line of defense. "Cavalry is at its worst when it's being outflanked," he said. "Don't kill ponies. Get the riders. Wild ponies only upset mounted men trying to charge. Dead ponies only serve as breastworks for such as are on foot."

"You tellin' me, Captain!" Q said, squinting over the sights of his rifle as he estimated range and windage. "I fought ag'in Phil Sheridan's Yank cavalry at Spotsylvania. You don't stop fightin' men by killin' horses. Them damned bluebellies fought afoot as hard as they did on hawsback. Ain't that right, Zeno?"

"Correct, grayback, except it was me that had to try to stand off Jeb Stuart an' that pack of crazy men what called themselves the best ca'vlrymen in the world," Zeno said.

"I keep forgittin' you was a bluebelly," Q said. "You almost act like a human bein' at times."

Parson Jones and Beaverslide had taken positions back of rock outcrops near each other. "Keep yore danged hat on, Beaverslide," the Parson said. "Leastways till the sun goes down. It shines so it'll bring the whole passel of 'em down on us two an' we'll have to handle it alone."

"I figure the best way is for you to rear up, start one of your hell-fire sermons an' talk 'em to death," Beaverslide said.

Ann Lansing and her mother, rifles in hands, crouched back of the barricades that had been set up against the wagons. With them was Rachel, who had armed herself with a huge muzzle-loading, single-shot blunderbuss. Clay did not know it had been in the wagons. She had Cindy at her side and was talking calmly to the child, assuring her that everything would be all right. Micah was hunkered in a firing position near them. So was Phil Lansing.

Bill Conners had squirmed to cover nearby. Phil Lansing spoke harshly to Clay. "What will we do with him?"

"Give him back his rifle," Clay said. "If he can't hit the back of a man who's standing still he likely won't be worth a hoot against warriors coming at him, but we'll at least give him a chance."

Lansing frowned. "He might not miss a fourth time."

"Meaning that he might cheat you out of your fun?" Clay asked.

Phil Lansing did not answer. Clay studied the mass of riders across the flat. The speech-making had ended. A battle line began to form. Indians moved to the left, and their guerrilla allies formed the right wing. Stone Buffalo could be seen toward the center. Evidently he had taken command in place of the fallen Major Blood.

Q spoke from his position. "No squaws, no camping stuff with the Injuns. That means this must be only a scouting or hunting party, riding ahead of the main bunch. There must be a lot more of 'em somewhere around."

"Let's hope the others don't get here until too late," Clay

said. "We might be able to hold off this bunch until dark and get a chance to wriggle away."

Nobody spoke. They knew that what Clay was saying was that it was now a case of saving their own lives, even if it meant abandoning the cattle they had driven so many hundreds of miles.

"Here they come!" Jem Rance shouted.

"Don't open up until I give the word," Clay warned.

The Indian-guerrilla charge was wild, primitive, and not too well organized. Red men screeched shrilly to intimidate their opponents. They brandished buffalo spears and hatchets in a promise of horrible death. Scalping knives were gripped in teeth; bronzed faces and dark eyes were ablaze with the threat of torture and agony.

The renegade whites were even more fearsome in aspect as they came charging to battle. They were yelling too, screeching obscene threats. Their bearded faces were aflame with the lust of expected conquest. They had seen the women. They expected easy slaughter, easy victory.

Around Clay rose a savage, shrill response to the challenge. The Rebel Yell, the battlecry of men in gray which had been the death knell of so many in the great war.

Clay joined in the Rebel Yell. Once again the conflicting emotions of battle were upon him, emotions he had hoped he would never have to endure again. He was torn by fear of death, and at the same time by the vengeful urge to shatter these humans who were seeking to kill him. One part of him kept urging him to turn and run, but the dominant part of him demanded that he stand fast and deal out what destruction he could to these foes who were challenging his fiber. He was torn between the urge to cower, and the eagerness to come to grips with these arrogant strangers.

He heard feminine voices around him joining in the Rebel Yell. Zeno, who had worn the blue, aided in that challenge. The battle fervor had gripped them all. The oncoming riders heard. Clay fancied that they had wavered for a moment. It was not the first time that sound had driven fear to attackers. Then they kept coming, but he was aware they were suddenly knowing doubt, and that this doubt might be greater than their thirst for captives and scalps. They were wondering now if they had not found a lion instead of a rabbit.

They were now so near that Clay could make out the lather on the ponies, the shine of grease on bronzed bodies.

"Fire!" he shouted.

He began shooting. He was battlewise, hardened by the terrors he had seen at Antietam, in the swamps around Vicksburg, in the blinding thickets of the Wilderness where friend fired upon friend by mistake. Around him other guns were crashing. The shooting was steady, restrained. Parson Jones, to Clay's right, was kneeling, taking time to follow his target carefully before pulling the trigger, then settling back to ram a new charge into his muzzle-loading Sharps. But, to his left, Lonnie Randall was emptying a Henry as fast as he could work the action.

"Slowly, son," Clay shouted. "Slowly. Pick your man and hold down on him."

He saw Beaverslide suddenly reel back and crumple into limpness. A sickness came upon him. He had seen so many go like that.

Jem Rance was hard hit. He staggered back, fell, then gamely got to his knees, picked up his rifle and began firing again.

Bill Conners was shooting frenziedly, the fear of death graying his face. Saddles of the attackers were being emptied and loose animals were running wildly, impeding the guerrillas and the red men. A heavy Comanche spear passed by Clay's head and thudded into the wooden side of the chuck wagon, splintering a plank.

The guerrillas broke, and their retreat spread to the Indians. What had really broken the charge was the gunfire from the flanks where Clay had stationed Q's brothers.

That and the blood-chilling Rebel Yell which was being carried high into the sky by the voices of women—women who were using rifles also.

The attackers fled out of range. Loose ponies wandered aimlessly among scattered bodies on the battlefield. Clay could hear the herd stampeding away in the distance.

The frenzy of battle faded. He became aware that he was still alive, still breathing. He was gasping for air, as though he had been in a long, heart-bursting race. This was a terrible sensation that had been all too familiar with him in the past on many battlefields. He sank down on hands and knees, gulping, unable to find the strength to arise for a time. Battle at close quarters had always drained him thus.

Women were weeping. Rose Lansing knelt beside the body of Beaverslide, wringing her hands. Ann and Rachel wept over another still form. This was the bluebelly, Zeno. A spear had been driven through the big man. Q stood looking down at Zeno, the same futile grief in his homely face that was driving Rose Lansing and the others. The alphabet quartet, Ace, Bass, Cass, and Des, joined him and had no words to say.

Micah moved in, lifted Zeno's body in his strong arms and carried him to a spread tarp, then brought Beaverslide to lie beside him. "Dey are both in de happy land now," he said. "Zeno's wid his family. Mr. Beaverslide kin tell how he fought a man's fight, an' he won't be tellin' a lie."

Parson Jones, gripping with his right hand an ugly bullet wound in his left forearm, stood over the body of Beaverslide, his comrade of many years, raised a rigid clenched fist, and said in a bitter voice, "Why? Why, O Lord? He believed in You. He lived by the Golden Rule. And now he is dead, and I, who have doubted You many times, am alive. Why?"

Micah was leading the women in prayer. Parson Jones bowed his head, sank to his knees, and prayed also.

Lonnie Randall was wounded. A slug from one of the

fearful, bell-mouthed *escopetes,* handed down through the tribes from the early Spanish days, had torn a gouge in the flesh of his left shoulder. Ann Lansing, with the help of Lonnie's father, doctored the injury from the medicine chest and bound it. She kissed Lonnie, and that did more for him than the medication.

Jem Rance and Ace had wounds, the first a bullet in the calf of his leg, and Ace with a shoulder slash from a Comanche knife in the hands of the only warrior who had managed to penetrate the wagon defense line. There the Indian had been shot dead. His body still lay near the wagon barricades. Rose Lansing and Rachel had fired simultaneously at this tragic red man who had tried to leap at them over the barricades. Neither would ever know which had fired the death shot, but neither would forget that moment as long as she lived. The Comanche had been very young, very handsome, very brave.

Clay assessed their losses, estimated their strength. They had won the first round, but at heavy cost. They had dealt fearful punishment. The bodies of five Comanches and three guerrillas lay on the field, and many more of the foe had been carried away wounded, and some dead, no doubt.

The guerrillas and the Indians had withdrawn farther into the prairie to where the gypsy circus had made its new camp. Silence came. The hot afternoon breeze drove away the acrid tang of powdersmoke, the smell of blood and death.

Clay helped carry Beaverslide and Zeno into the nearby wash where graves were dug. He stood while the Parson read the sad and achingly lonely words: "Ashes to ashes, dust to dust." They caved a cutbank over the tarp-wrapped bodies, marked the spot for future reference, and went back to care for the wounded and to fight for the living.

In the distance Clay listened to the lamentation of warriors, mourning the dead. Buzzards soared over the battlefield, but the Texas men cursed them and drove them away with thrown rocks. Comanches and guerrillas came under

white flags, and the defenders lay silent and let them
carry away the bodies.

The hot afternoon waned, dusk moved in, and the mauve
shadows deepened. The attack had not been resumed, but
it was evident that the foe was not in the mood to withdraw.

"They're waiting for the main bunch to come up," Q said.

His prediction was soon confirmed. A new commotion
arose in the twilight. Clay climbed onto a wagon, peering.
The reinforcements that Q had foreseen, were arriving in
the camp of the allies. He could see many ponies, many
riders, many travois approaching. Soon he could hear the
wailing of squaws joining in the ceremonies for the dead.

"Ain't there an Army fort somewhere in these parts?"
Jess Randall asked.

"None in more than a hundred miles, according to the
map," Clay said reluctantly.

"A hundred miles? We'd all be dead before we could get
to them an' back—if we could git out at all."

Phil Lansing spoke. "I passed a big company of freighters
yesterday down the trail. They came from San'tone and are
heading for Leavenworth, loaded with leather and such
truck. They had a troop of Union cavalry with them as an
escort, but they didn't look like they needed it. There must
have been fifty wagons in the outfit, manned by tough
whackers and swampers, most of whom likely had been
soldiers not long ago."

"Where?" Clay exclaimed. "When?"

"Two days ago," Lansing said. "That was about fifty miles
south, I reckon, but they were heading north. Likely they
might be only fifteen, twenty miles away by this time,
camping on a stream I crossed this morning."

Hope soared. Then it faded. "They might as well be on
the moon," the Parson said. "Nobody's goin' to git out of
this fix. Them devils out there are likely expectin' somethin'
like that. They're already spreadin' all around us. They're
in the wash, both above an' below us, an' acrost from us."

There was silence. The slow darkness was settling. The knowledge was in the minds of every man that if help was to arrive in time the messenger must be soon on his way.

From the darkness came a burst of sound, the thudding footsteps of a running man, the faint pad of moccasined feet, the crash of disturbed brush. A scream came. It was the despairing sound from a frenzied human. A struggle was taking place down the dry wash. More strangled outcries came, then faded.

Clay peered around. "Where's Conners?"

Bill Conners was no longer among them. He had seized a chance to attempt to creep away. Faint sounds came for a time. Then, nearer at hand, a man began moaning in torture in the darkness. The moaning increased. Horrible screaming came.

Ann Lansing covered her ears, sank to her knees. Her mother tried to comfort her. From the darkness, savage, taunting voices arose, laughing, jeering, mocking, promising in Spanish, broken English, and dialect the same fate for all of them.

Presently silence came again. It was over—for Bill Conners, at least. But not for the Patchsaddle crew. The taunting and the promises of torture and death for them were resumed by the warriors and guerrillas in the darkness. They tried not to listen, but that was impossible. They had no doubts about the vigilance of the foes who surrounded them. The voices came from all points. Nor were there any doubts as to the torture that awaited any, like Conners, who were taken alive.

Clay broke the bitter silence around him. "Someone has to get through to that wagon train and fetch help."

Again the silence. No face was turned toward him. None wanted to look at him, to be placed in the position of forcing the decision on him. But the decision had to be made.

Once again he was thinking of that day at a stream whose waters had been turned to crimson when the loneliness of command had been a spike in his heart, a spike that had never been removed. That was the day he had sent Phil Lansing and eleven other men to what seemed like sure death. Now he was living it over again.

He looked at Phil Lansing. "Two of us must try it," he said. "Two strings to the bow. We'd have a better chance of success. Remember Hatcher's Run, Sergeant? Remember how two hundred men lived and ten died to save them? Remember how it was done? I made the decision that day. Now it's your turn. These are your flesh and blood, your neighbors, your friends. There's only two who should go. You name them."

CHAPTER 13

Phil Lansing stared at him for long seconds, a bitter trapped hopelessness in his eyes. "You can't do this to me, Burnet," he almost whispered.

"You have no choice and you know it," Clay said. "I'll be one to try it. I'm unhurt, strong. There's only one other person among us who is uninjured, young, strong enough to have a chance of making it through. You can't go. Your leg. This has to be done by persons who can move fast and have endurance. The rest of you will have to make a diversion so as to draw them away long enough for us to slip through. It will be a diversion like you and Joe Owens and ten other men made that day at Hatcher's Run to save me and two hundred other soldiers."

Phil Lansing did not speak for a space. His face was gray, without trace of life or blood. "It worked that day," he said with an effort. "It just might work again. Damn you to hell, Burnet. I wish now I'd never come out of it alive that day."

"The rest of you will start shooting and act like you're stampeding down the wash in an attempt to break out," Clay said. "That might draw them all there while we make a try for it in the opposite direction. We might head for their camp, for that could be the one direction they're likely to leave open, figuring nobody will try it."

There was a silence. "Who's to go with you?" the Parson finally asked reluctantly. "I ought to be the one. I'm strong, an' unhurt, an' I'm mighty spry."

Every able man in the group spoke up, volunteering. But Clay did not speak. He was looking at Phil Lansing, waiting.

"You've got no right to put this on me, Burnet," Lansing said, his voice mirroring the torture inside him. "I'll kill you for this, if for nothing else, if we both live."

He looked at his sister. "You're the one, Ann," he said huskily. "The others, like Micah, are too big, too clumsy, or they're old or wounded, or crippled like—like me. You're young, strong, quick."

"Of course," she said calmly above a chorus of protest from the men. "I knew that from the first."

"God forgive me," her brother said.

Rose Lansing kissed her daughter. "You will come back to us, darling. I know that. I feel it. Our prayers will go with you."

Her brother spoke hoarsely. "Ann, if they catch you . . ." He could not bring himself to finish it.

"I know what to do," she said with that same calmness.

Clay sat on the ground and began pulling off his boots. "You do the same," he told Ann. "We'll make less noise in socks. Hang your boots around your neck. We'll black our faces from the cook pots."

He gave his rifle to Phil Lansing, along with what spare ammunition he had for the long gun and his six-shooter. "I'll keep my sidegun," he said. "Extra shells won't do us any good if luck runs against us and they might be more needed here. You're in charge now."

He drew Ann into his arms and kissed her. "At least we'll be together, no matter what happens," he said.

"Yes," she said, weeping a little. "Oh, yes, my darling."

Clay released her and spoke to the others. "Mrs. Lansing and Rachel and Cindy should stay with the wagons. The rest of you begin yelling and shooting. Make a big commotion, as though you're on your way down the draw. Then drop flat in case they open fire, and slowly work your way back to the wagons. But keep yelling all the time to hold them."

He waited for suggestions. None came. "Now," he said. "The sooner we start, the better."

The attempt at a diversion began. The men ran to the rim of the wash and dropped into it. They began yelling and crashing through brush, creating what uproar they could. Grasping Ann's hand, Clay left the barricades and they scuttled on hands and knees into the open. Starlight seemed agonizingly bright in the sky. He heard Ann breathing hard and knew that she entertained terrible fear.

The glow from the distant campfires of the attackers lifted a faint crimson curtain, outlining the crest of a low swell ahead. Shadows were moving fast there. Indians and guerrillas, some on foot, some mounted. They were all speeding like mannequins in a mad puppet show across their route, heading toward the uproar in the stream bed.

They flattened out and did not move until the puppets had cavorted past. Then they began squirming frantically ahead. The Patchsaddle men were performing their task nobly. The pandemonium behind them was increasing. Guns began to explode.

Clay led the way, seeking to avoid what obstacles he could on the rough terrain. He paused abruptly, again pressing Ann flat to the ground. Someone ran past them scarcely a rod away. Clay judged that he was a guerrilla because of his heavy, booted tread. The man vanished in the direction of the uproar.

They moved again. They crested the low rise and the encampment was in sight within rifleshot ahead. Cookfires burned there and they could make out the squaws moving about, staring, talking, and gesticulating.

They circled far away from this danger. They chanced getting on their feet, but ran crouching to avoid being sky-lined. The snuffle and stir of horses ahead warned them in time that they were moving toward the big herd of ponies on graze beyond the camp of their foes, and they were forced to veer far wide of this peril also.

"If we could only steal horses . . ." Ann said in an excited whisper.

"Too dangerous," Clay said. "They'll be guarded."

They put more distance between them and the crimson glow. "All right," Clay said. "I think we're out of the frying pan, at least. Faster!"

They straightened and began running. They ran until they could run no more, then fell flat, their lungs laboring. Clay's agony eased, and he listened. All sounds had died back of them. The diversion attempt had died of attrition. By this time the guerrillas and Stone Buffalo would know that it had been a trick, and that someone likely had managed to steal out of the trap. There would be pursuit.

"Not even a Comanche can find our trail in the dark," Ann said hopefully.

Clay said nothing. Presently they heard the dogs—a far, heart-freezing sound, a shrill, coyotelike screeching.

"Dear God!" Ann sobbed. "Help us now!" They began running again.

They suddenly found themselves among cattle. They had blundered upon a remnant of their own scattered Patchsaddle drive. A horned animal loomed in their path. Clay was caught by a wild inspiration.

"Up!" he panted. "Ride 'em, cowgirl."

He lifted Ann off her feet. Before she realized his intention she found herself astride a Longhorn. In the next moment Clay joined her aboard the startled creature. Luck was with them, for their mount was a cow, one of the smaller animals in their herd. Even so it was a Longhorn with its share of strength and wildness.

Ann clung to the spread of horns and Clay clung to her. The cow was too dumbfounded to move for an instant. Then it took off with a wild snort of terror. Its flight set off a stampede among other cattle nearby in the darkness.

The cow ran blindly for a short distance, then began to rid itself of its burden. It sunfished, swapped ends, and the girl and Clay went sailing. They crashed into a clump of brush that cushioned their fall and lay there in a tangle of arms and legs. The stampede thundered away into the blackness of the night.

Clay scrambled to his feet. "Are you hurt?" he asked.

"No," she gasped. Then she began to laugh hysterically. "Ride 'em, cowgirl. I tried my best."

He drew her to her feet. They could still hear the ululation of dogs in the distance. Clay was sure that any chance the dogs might have had of trailing them was ended now, wiped out by the stampede of cattle.

They headed southward again. Phil Lansing had estimated that the wagon train encampment would be on a stream where the Patchsaddle herd had bedded on its last camp, some fifteen miles away at the speed a cattle drive normally travels. Their route was easy to follow, even in darkness, marked by the cropping of grass and the droppings of cattle.

They had donned their boots earlier during a breather, but cowboots were not intended for this sort of use. Clay knew that his feet were blistering, and he was sure Ann was suffering the same misery. Neither mentioned it.

Clay estimated the time was nearing midnight, according to the position of the Dipper, when he caught the acrid tang of herded livestock. They followed this downwind until they were challenged by a sentry. Beyond, lay the scattered night fires of an enormous camp, ringed by the towering hoods of freight wagons.

The sentry was a lank young soldier who told them to advance and be identified, and who shouted for the sergeant of the guard. To his consternation, the trooper found himself being kissed by one of the ragged, breathless arrivals.

"Hurry, soldier!" Clay said. "We're from a trail crew

that's in bad trouble ahead. I want to talk to your commander."

The commander was a lieutenant, a West Pointer, who was groggy with sleep, and confused. "You say you were an officer in the rebe—I mean the Confederate forces?" he mumbled, trying to pull on his jacket and stuff his shirt into hastily donned trousers as he realized he was in the presence of a member of the opposite sex.

"That war's over," Clay said. "We're in another one, and you'll soon see action, Lieutenant."

Soon he was in the saddle heading north. Back of them rode the lieutenant's detachment of thirty troopers. Reinforcing them were that many more men from the freight caravan, tough mule skinners, hardened swampers and game hunters, all of whom knew how to use guns. The majority had served in one army or the other during the war.

Ann rode with them. She had scorned the lieutenant's objections and laughed at his doubts as to whether she could stand the hardships of the return trip. "After what I've been through I could ride all the way to Missouri and back," she said.

Clay watched the first small radiance of dawn in the sky. "Faster, Lieutenant!" he said. "Faster, for God's sake! It's coming! Daybreak! We'll be too late!"

Full dawn came. The miles that had seemed endless to him on foot in the darkness were visible miles now, and even more endless. The horses and mules on which the motley aggregation was mounted were beginning to tire under the hard pace.

Clay stood up in the stirrups and said hoarsely, "Hear it?"

The lieutenant could hear nothing, but a civilian scout in buckskins who had been riding ahead, along with three Pawnees, returned, with his horse at a gallop to report. "Fight goin' on ahead, Lieutenant. Guns talkin'."

The Lieutenant ordered his followers ahead faster. Clay,

forcing his horse into the lead, was first to come in sight of the fight.

A pony charge by the reinforced Indians was forming and it was evident that the wagon camp was sure to be overrun. Stone Buffalo's warriors were unaware that help had arrived. They were moving in a long double line toward the barricaded camp, warriors hanging on the far sides of the ponies, preparing to ride down the defenders.

Stone Buffalo gave the signal and the ponies broke into a gallop. The charge became thunder and color and ferocity. Clay's appearance was the first intimation that Stone Buffalo had of danger. Other warriors turned too, staring, and now the head of the oncoming column of cavalry and wagon men could be seen.

The bulk of the pony charge continued for a moment. Clay, riding to the wagons, was caught in a melee of ponies and warriors, some of whom were wheeling to face the new threat, and others still intent on their original targets.

Around him guns were exploding, and Indians were screeching amid terrible confusion. Clay found himself falling. His horse had been killed by a bullet. Stone Buffalo loomed above him, a spear aloft to skewer him. A bullet struck the chief. The spear thrust wavered and weakened. It missed Clay, the heavy metal head burying itself in the earth at his side.

It was Phil Lansing who had fired the shot. Clay looked at him, and he knew that it was over. The feud, the hatreds, the misunderstandings. Over forever. He got to his feet and they stood side by side to meet further challenge.

But the battle was also over. With Stone Buffalo fallen, and the odds evened, the guerrillas had already deserted their allies, and the Indians were forced to flee. Warriors were riding back to their camp where they were being joined by the squaws in a flight that was successful, for the horses and mules of the arrivals were in no condition for pursuit after the night's ride.

The lieutenant called off the chase. He returned and dismounted. He stared at Rose Lansing and at Rachel and Cindy. "What did you say you called this outfit?" he asked Clay.

"The Patchsaddle drive," Clay said. "Seven weeks out of the San Dimas country, with a mixed herd of twenty-five hundred head of beef. Leastwise we had that many when we set out. I don't know how many we'll tally now, if any at all."

The officer continued to gaze around disbelievingly. The Parson was binding the wounds of Q, who had fought hand to hand with a Comanche, whom he had disarmed and then had permitted to ride away. The brothers Ace and Bass were standing over the body of Des, who had been struck down by an arrow. Cindy was with them, and all were weeping. Strong men do not weep?

"And where are these cattle now?" the lieutenant asked.

"Around somewhere, what's left of 'em," Clay said. "We could use a little help rounding them up. We're on our way to find end of steel in the state of Missouri. We're not sure how far away it is."

"Only another hundred miles or so," the officer said, still acting as though he was dreaming. "It happens we're on our way there also. We'll ride along with you. Rounding up cattle isn't exactly in our line, but we'll give it a try."

The shipping point was a settlement called Springfield in Missouri. The railroad had reached Springfield, and engineers and surveyors were there, preparing to help extend the line on into Kansas and The Nations. The town had changed from a collection of log houses into a hell-on-wheels, with all the attractions, including women.

"Painted hussies!" Rose Lansing sniffed. She sat in a rocking chair in the upper parlor of the best rooming house the town afforded. She wore a new dress. It was of economical cotton, for she had resisted her daughter's urging to buy silk.

On the bed lay gunnysacks containing some thirty-eight thousand dollars in gold coin. Buyers had been waiting at Springfield with cash, for beef was at a premium in eastern packing houses, and the Patchsaddle drive had been one of the first to arrive. The herd had tallied out at nineteen hundred and ten head of the original twenty-five hundred and had brought twenty dollars a head. The San Dimas men would return home with more cash in their wallets than they had ever seen in their lives.

Clay and Phil Lansing were in the room, rifles and side-guns handy. Lonnie Randall, recovered from his wound, was there also, sitting in a corner, gloomily listening to the sounds of revelry that drifted from the street. The Patch-saddle crew was celebrating.

Rose Lansing had been prevailed on to advance fifty dollars to each man from the Patchsaddle stake so that the members could shake the saddle kinks out of their "laigs," as the Parson put it. The shaking was well started. Night had fallen, and the drinks were flowing freely. For all except Lonnie. Rose Lansing had firmly refused to let him join the hurrah. "You just stay put where I can keep an eye on you, young man," she had said.

Ann was in the room also, along with Rachel and Cindy. They wore new, comely garb which they had bought on a shopping spree at Springfield's newly stocked stores.

Rose Lansing arose and brought into view a sizable object, covered by a piece of wagon sheet. She stood in front of Clay and removed the cover. It was the homemade easel on which he had been working the day it had all started back in the San Dimas. She placed on the easel the half-finished landscape he had been attempting.

"Now you can go ahead with it in peace," she said.

Clay kissed her. "Would you object to having a Burnet as a son-in-law?" he asked.

"It's about time," she said. "Fact is, that is one of the

things I had in mind right from the start when I rode over to your place that day."

Ann sprang to her feet. "Well, if that isn't the damnedest proposal I ever heard of. Only a coward would go to a girl's mother and—"

She got no further, being crushed in Clay's arms. "Just because you're a tough trail hand doesn't give you the right to do any cussing," he told her. "Mind me now."

F
FARR
Farrell
Patchsaddle drive

WCPL ✗

NOV 1 4 1992

JUL 2 - 1993

MAY 1 7 1995

AUG 1 2 2000

DISCARDED BY THE LEVI
HEYWOOD MEMORIAL LIBRARY

NOV 9 1972

3 3945 0001 7